To My
Three Friends

BERYL BRAITHWAITE
JAMES ANNAND
and
LOU SNIDER

who have worked with me since
the day "Maggie Muggins" was "born"
this book is fondly dedicated

Maggie Muggins

AND MR. McGARRITY

by

MARY GRANNAN

Illustrations by

PAT. PATIENCE

THOMAS ALLEN & SON LIMITED

TORONTO • VANCOUVER

FIRST PUBLISHED 1952
THOMAS ALLEN LTD., TORONTO

FIRST PAPERBACK EDITION
© THOMAS ALLEN & SON LIMITED 1985
MARKHAM, ONTARIO

Canadian Cataloguing in Publication Data

Grannan, Mary, 1900—1975
    Maggie Muggins and Mr. McGarrity

Stories based on radio programmes broadcast on CBC.
ISBN 0-919028-67-5

1. Children's stories, Canadian (English).*
2. Canadian fiction (English) — 20th century.*
I. Patience, Pat.   II. Title.

PS8513.R36M33 1952   jC813'.52   C52-1019
PZ7. G73Ma 1952

A limited edition Maggie Muggins Doll
in porcelain by April Katz is available
from the Dolly Madison Doll Company
5336 Yonge Street, Willowdale, Ontario
M2N 5P9

Printed in Canada by
T.H. Best Printing Company Ltd.
Don Mills, Ontario

The Stories

BIG BITE'S MISTAKE

Maggie Muggins is fun, and she has freckles on her nose, and it's turned up, and she has two pigtails the colour of brand new carrots, and she has a friend named Mr. McGarrity. He works in a garden, and days when Maggie can't think of a thing to do he always thinks of something, and he knows where the violets grow in the springtime, and he knows where the red-headed woodpeckers nest. And I'll never forget the time he showed Maggie the butterflies gilding their wings. Maggie watched those butterflies most all of a day . . . and now, here comes Maggie Muggins herself. She's dancing down the garden path, and she's singing,

> "*Tra la, la la, la la, la luggins,*
>   *Here comes Maggie, Maggie Muggins.*
>   *And I am coming tra la, la lo*
>   *Just to say a glad 'hello' to Mr.*
>   *McGarrity.*"

"Hello, Mr. McGarrity."

The kindly old man, who was working in his cucumber bed, leaned on his red-handled hoe and laughed. "Hello yourself, Maggie Muggins," he said, "and how goes the day with you?"

"Oh pretty well, sir," answered the little freckled-faced girl. "How goes it with you?"

"Pretty well, too," said Mr. McGarrity.

"That makes us both 'pretty and well', doesn't it?" said Maggie.

Mr. McGarrity laughed again. "I don't know about the 'pretty', Maggie," he said. "I've never thought of myself as pretty."

"I have," said Maggie, tossing her red head. "I've thought of you that way. I think you're the prettiest and nicest 'Mr. McGarrity' in the world."

Mr. McGarrity then made pretend that she was a Queen, whose word was law, and he bowed low before her.

"Thank you very much, Miss Muggins. I thank you, and so does my red-handled hoe." And Mr. McGarrity made pretend that the hoe was bowing to Maggie too.

Maggie told Mr. McGarrity and the red-handled hoe that they were both most welcome and then, looking a little anxiously into the face of the old gardener, she said, "And what do you think of me, sir, now that I've told you what I think of you?"

Mr. McGarrity's eyes were twinkling as he replied, "I think you're the prettiest and the nicest 'Maggie Muggins' in all the world and, by the way, what is 'the prettiest and nicest Maggie Muggins in all the world' going to do today?"

"Would you really like to know, sir?" asked Maggie.

"Upon my word, that is a stupid question! Of course I want to know," said Mr. McGarrity.

"Well," said Maggie, hopping around the red-handled hoe on one foot, "I'll tell you. You know Big Bite Beaver, Mr. McGarrity?"

"I know him very well, and a fine fellow he is, too," said Mr. McGarrity.

"Yes, isn't he though? He's one of my best friends, and I'll tell you the because-why. He's kind and he's good and he likes me. And do you know what he's going to do today, Mr. McGarrity?"

The old man shook his head, and Maggie went on. "He's going to move his house."

"No!" said Mr. McGarrity.

"Yes, he's going to move his house. He thinks he needs a change, and you know that stream along the railway track?"

This time Mr. McGarrity nodded his head.

"Well," Maggie said, "Big Bite's building a new beaver dam there, and do you know the because-why of that?"

"I couldn't even guess the 'because-why' of that," laughed Mr. McGarrity.

"He wants to see the trains going by," and Maggie laughed too.

4

"Well upon my word, who ever would think that Big Bite would want to see the trains going by?"

"Yes, who ever would . . . I mean I would, because I know, because he told me so," said Maggie Muggins.

Mr. McGarrity cocked his head to one side, half closed his merry eyes, bit his lower lip in deep thought, and then said, "I hope Big Bite doesn't get into any trouble."

"Big Bite never gets into any trouble," said Maggie. "He's a good beaver."

"I know, I know, but about moving his house along the railway tracks! I'm not quite sure that it's a good idea."

Maggie's face darkened and Mr. McGarrity, seeing this, said, "There, there, it's nothing to worry about. You run along and watch Big Bite build his new dam."

"Yes, sir," said Maggie, brightening again. "And I'll tell you all about it when I see you again."

Maggie danced away then, through the cabbage patch, past the scarlet runners, under the hedge and off into the green fields beyond. She was going to the little pink mouse house in the meadow, where her friend Fitzgerald would be waiting for her. Petunia

5

'possum was there also. Petunia waved from the front window as Maggie dashed up the walk.

"Hello, Petunia! Hello, Fitzgerald," Maggie called out in greeting.

"Hello, Maggie Muggins, and how are you, if I may ask?" said the little mouse, with a merry twinkle in his tiny beady eyes. He knew how Maggie was. He could tell by looking at her that she was feeling fine and ready for adventure.

"Are you ready to go over to the railway tracks to watch Big Bite build his new house?" Maggie asked of her two friends.

"Almost, but not quite," said the fieldmouse.

Maggie pretended to sigh. "I know what the 'not quite' is," she said. "You've made a song about Big Bite's new house, haven't you?"

"How ever did you guess?" laughed Fitzgerald, as he went to the tiny grand piano in the corner of his pretty little living room.

Fitzgerald arranged the piano stool to suit him, draped his handsome long tail over it, and began to sing to the tune of an old folk song,

> *"Big Bite's working by the railroad,*
> *To build himself a house,*
> *And someone is going to watch him,*
> *That someone is a mouse.*

6

And the little mouse is pretty,
He's got a fine long tail
And some very handsome whiskers,
Which you'll see by the rail . . . road,
If you go down there to watch Big
Bite working."

Fitzgerald swung around on the piano stool with a mischievous glint in his eyes. Maggie Muggins tossed a nearby sofa cushion at him and laughingly said, "That's certainly a lovely song about Big Bite. Of all the conceited mice I've ever met, you're certainly the worst."

Fitzgerald burst out laughing now, and said, "Yes, I am."

"I'm glad that you know it," said Maggie. "Well, 'Fine Long Tail and Handsome Whiskers', are you ready to go to the tracks now?"

"Yes," said Fitzgerald. "Come on, Petunia. Get up off the chesterfield and let's go."

And away they went . . . Maggie, Petunia, and the still laughing little mouse. As they neared the woodland directly west of the railway track, they saw Big Bite Beaver waiting for them. They called out to him in greeting and then Maggie said, "Big Bite, haven't you started your new dam yet?"

"No, Maggie," said the big fellow with a toothy smile. "I was waiting for you. I thought you'd like to see me cutting down that tree over there. It's going to be the beginning of my new dam."

Maggie's eyes followed the direction in which Big Bite's paw was pointing. She cried out in amazement, "That tree! Big Bite, can you cut down that tree?"

"Sure he can," said Fitzgerald, "Big Bite can cut down any tree, can't you, Big Bite?"

"Well, I . . . I . . . suppose I can," said the beaver, blushing a little. "Yes . . . I . . . I suppose I could if I tried, but I don't want to try. I just cut down trees that I need, and I need that one. I'm going to start cutting now."

The beaver sunk his sharp teeth into the trunk of the tree. The chips began to fly, and the sound of Big Bite's teeth in the wood sounded almost like an electric drill.

"My gracious, Aunt Matilda," gasped Maggie Muggins. "Just look at him. Just look at those chips."

Big Bite stopped suddenly and went around to the other side of the tree.

"Where are you going, Big Bite?" asked Petunia 'possum.

"I'm going to cut on the other side of the trunk now," said Big Bite. "When I cut through the other side, the tree will fall down." He went to work again with vim and, in a few minutes he called out: "Run, run . . . the tree's going to fall."

"Timber!" squealed Fitzgerald in delight.

"Oh, Oh," cried Maggie. "Look, look at the way the tree is falling! It's going to fall across the tracks."

"Lan' sakes, Honey Chil', it is across the track. Now what we done do?" gasped Petunia.

And at that very minute the sound of an approaching train could be heard. Its whistle echoed across the woodland.

Maggie's face paled as the train whistle grew louder. "We've got to do something," she cried. "The train will be wrecked if we don't get that big tree off the track, and we can't get the tree off the track, because we're not strong enough, so we've got to stop the train."

"But how can we do that, Maggie, how, how?" cried Fitzgerald. There was no laughter in the little mouse now. He saw the danger in the situation. And then Maggie had an idea. It wasn't much of a one, she knew that, but it was the best she could do

9

in a hurry, so she said, "I'll take my hat off, and I'll wave it, and my hair is red, and 'red' means stop."

"I'll wave my tail too, Maggie," said Fitzgerald, eager to be of help.

Maggie couldn't help smiling at that, and she told the little mouse that it was good of him to think of it, but that she was afraid that his tail would not be seen. "But we mustn't talk any more. We've no time to waste. Come on."

Big Bite, Fitzgerald, and Petunia followed Maggie Muggins as she ran in the direction of the fallen tree, past it and up the track. There she stood, waving her hat and her red pigtails, and screaming at the top of her voice, "Stop! Stop! Danger ahead!"

The driver of the locomotive saw the frantic Maggie and her more than frantic animal friends and, sensing that something was wrong, he brought his train to a quick stop. He climbed down from the cab of the engine and, in a few minutes, the passengers came swarming down from the cars.

Although they were all grateful to Maggie for saving their lives, they were very angry at Big Bite for cutting down the tree, which might have meant disaster to them. They all began to talk at once, blaming the beaver for what he had done. Big Bite, near to tears, tried to make himself heard above the din.

"But, my goodness! But, my goodness!" he kept saying over and over. "But, my goodness, listen to me, please. I didn't mean that the tree should fall on the tracks. Really and truly, I didn't! Tell them I didn't, Maggie," he said, turning to his little friend.

But the angry crowd would not listen to Maggie now, either. They kept blaming Big Bite. Between them they managed to pull the offending tree from the track, and the train was ready to roll again. In a little while it was on its way, but the conductor had taken Big Bite along. He was going to hand Big Bite over to the police. He said that Big Bite was guilty of wilfully obstructing traffic and endangering lives. A frightened and bewildered Maggie Muggins ran back to the garden to Mr. McGarrity.

That old gentleman looked up from his work and said, "Well, upon my word, Maggie Muggins, you do look worried. What has happened?"

"Oh, Mr. McGarrity! Oh, Mr. McGarrity!" panted Maggie. "I'm worse than worried, I'm . . . I'm scared. Mr. McGarrity, he got into it."

Mr. McGarrity laughed and, leaning on his red-

11

handled hoe, he told Maggie to calm down and tell him what was the matter. "Who got into what, Maggie? Tell me that first."

"Big Bite got into trouble. You said he would, and he did," sobbed Maggie. "Oh, Mr. McGarrity, he should never have started to build a house by the railway tracks."

Mr. McGarrity raised his eyebrows in concern as he waited for Maggie to go on with her story.

"He's in jail, Mr. McGarrity. Big Bite Beaver is in jail. And, Mr. McGarrity, it wasn't his fault. He didn't mean it should fall on the tracks." And Maggie burst into a fresh flood of tears.

Mr. McGarrity shook the little girl, and said, "Come now, none of that. Stop moaning and groaning and tell me what fell on the tracks."

"A tree," said Maggie, "a big tree. You see, Mr. McGarrity, Big Bite didn't begin to build his dam until Fitzgerald and Petunia and I went over to watch him. He cut down the big tree with his teeth and it fell right across the railway tracks and then, Mr. McGarrity, I heard the train coming, and I knew I had to stop it, so I ran down the track and waved my red pigtails for a stop-light."

"No," laughed the old gardener.

"Yes," said Maggie, "as a stop-light, and the train stopped, and the train man got down and all the people got out, and they blamed Big Bite, Mr. McGarrity, and they took him off to jail."

"Well, upon my word," said Mr. McGarrity. "I never did hear tell of the like. I should think that they'd have been so glad that they were saved from a wreck that they'd have forgiven Big Bite for his mistake."

Maggie nodded her head. "They were glad they were saved, but they were angry too, and, Mr. McGarrity, what am I going to do? How am I going to get Big Bite out of jail?"

Mr. McGarrity gave the matter a little thought. Then he snapped his fingers and smiled broadly. "You're going to call up the Chief of the Police, Maggie, and you're going to tell him the whole story. Tell him that Big Bite didn't mean to let the tree fall on the tracks. Tell him that, although beavers can cut down trees, they cannot direct the way the trees are going to fall. Tell him those things, and tell him too, that Big Bite won't try again to build a new home near the railway, but that he'll go back to his old house in the woodland as soon as he is free."

"Yes, sir. Thank you, sir," said Maggie, "but,

13

Mr. McGarrity, do you think the Chief of Police will free Big Bite?"

"Of course he will," said Mr. McGarrity. "The police always free innocent people."

"And beavers?" asked the anxious Maggie.

"And beavers," said Mr. McGarrity.

Maggie found that Mr. McGarrity was right about the Chief of the Police. He listened carefully to Maggie's story, and told Maggie that she could come at once and sign Big Bite out. Maggie, along with her waiting friends, did this. It was music to Big Bite's ears when he heard the big iron key turning in his cell lock. His head was hanging and his paddle tail was dragging as he came out through the door.

"Big Bite Beaver," said Maggie sternly, "get a smile on that face of yours. You've got nothing to be ashamed of. It was just a mistake. Now come on and let's have some fun."

They all had fun, and then Maggie went back to the garden to Mr. McGarrity.

"I guess all is well again, Maggie Muggins," her old friend said to her as she came dancing into the carrot bed to him.

"Yes, sir, the Chief of Police was nice and kind, and Big Bite is free again. He felt sad but I told him that it was just a mistake, and anyone can make a mistake, can't he, Mr. McGarrity."

"He can indeed," smiled Mr. McGarrity. "Well, Maggie, all in all I'd say you'd had quite a day."

"Yes, because tra la, la la, la la, la lack, Big Bite dropped a tree on the railroad track. I don't know what will happen tomorrow."

SWORDS AND PINCERS

Maggie Muggins opened her eyes bright, early, and looked out on a beautiful morning.

"Hello, Day," she said, as she scrambled out of bed to make herself ready for her usual trip to the

16

garden. In a very few minutes she had had her bath, her breakfast, and was on her way singing,

> "*Tra la, la la, la la, la lee,*
> *Here comes Maggie Muggins me,*
> *And I am hopping lipperty larrety,*
> *To say 'hello' to Mr. McGarrity,*
> *And hello, Mr. McGarrity.*"

Mr. McGarrity, who had seen her dancing down the garden path, waved his red-handled hoe at her and said in answer to her merry greeting, "Hello yourself, Maggie Muggins, and how are you today?"

"I'm fine and good," said the little girl, "and how are you, sir?"

"Oh, I can't complain," answered her friend with a broad smile, "No, I can't complain."

"You wouldn't complain anyway, Mr. McGarrity, because 'complaining' means sort of sad growling, doesn't it?" said Maggie. "And you wouldn't 'sad growl', sir."

"Thank you very much, Miss Muggins," laughed the old man. "I try not to 'sad growl'. It's a very nice day, isn't it?" Mr. McGarrity went on to say. "And what, if I may ask, are you going to do with it?"

Maggie's freckled face puckered a little. She rolled her bright blue eyes and squeezed her apple-red lips, and then she said, "I haven't made up my mind yet what I'm going to do with this lovely day. Mr. McGarrity, do you think you could make up my mind for me?"

Mr. McGarrity shook his kindly grey head. "Dear me, what a lazy young lady we have here this morning, but I'll see what I can do for you. Mind you, I'll not make your mind up completely, but I'll give you a few hints on what you might do."

"All right, sir, I can take hints as easy as easy," said Maggie, beginning to hop around Mr. McGarrity's red-handled hoe on one foot. "What's the first hint?"

"It must be an exciting hint, I take it?" said Mr. McGarrity.

"Oh, yes, sir."

"Umm," said Mr. McGarrity. "Well now, when 'Jack the Nimble, Jack the Quick' wanted excitement, he jumped over the candle stick."

Maggie shook her head. "I don't think I'd like that and, besides, I haven't got a candle stick."

Mr. McGarrity laughed. "That does present a problem, doesn't it? You certainly can't jump over the candle stick if you haven't got a candle stick. I'll

18

try again. When Bobby Shaftoe wanted excitement 'Bobby Shaftoe went to sea, silver buckles on his knee', but I suppose you haven't got any silver buckles either?"

"No, sir, but it doesn't matter, sir, that I haven't, and you needn't try to think up anything else, because that's what I'll do today. I'll go to sea without silver buckles on my knee. I haven't seen Mr. Whale for the longest time, sir."

"That's right, you haven't seen him in a great while. I'm sure he'd be delighted if you called on him today. But, Maggie, Mr. Whale doesn't come in very close to the shore and there's no boat down there, if I remember correctly."

"You remember correctly, Mr. McGarrity, but you forget that I have a friend who is just as good as a boat any day," said Maggie.

"Of course, of course," said the old gardener. "You mean Big Bite Beaver, don't you, Maggie Muggins?"

Maggie nodded, and smiled proudly. "He lets me sit on his back, sir, and Petunia 'possum sits on my knee, and Fitzgerald Fieldmouse sits in Petunia's pocket ... and then Big Bite swims away, away, away with us."

19

Mr. McGarrity's merry eyes twinkled as he said seriously, "I can't think of a more delightful way to travel."

"Neither can I," agreed Maggie. "I'll take your love to Mr. Whale, sir, . . . that is, if you'd like me to do that."

"I'd be most obliged if you would, Maggie. Now off with you, and don't waste another minute of this lovely day," said Mr. McGarrity.

And off went Maggie toward the meadow and the pink mouse house where her good friend the fieldmouse lived. She knew that he and Petunia would be delighted, also, to see Mr. Whale. She hoped that Big Bite would feel the same way because, without Big Bite, they would have to postpone their visit until it suited him.

Petunia suggested that Maggie call Big Bite on the telephone right away to see if their plans were agreeable to him.

"Yes," said Fitzgerald, "and while you're talking on the telephone, I'll make up a 'whale' song."

Maggie laughed and shook her finger at the mouse. "As if we didn't know you'd make up a song! Hurry with it, because it's not going to take me long to find out from Big Bite if he can take us or not."

Maggie went to the tiny telephone and dialled "BEAVER 1234". In a few seconds she heard her woodland friend picking up the receiver. Maggie said, "Hello, this is Maggie Muggins, Big Bite. Are you very busy today? . . . Oh, I'm glad, because, Big Bite, we'd like you to take us to see Mr. Whale. . . . Oh, thank you, I knew you would if you had the time. . . . Well, yes, we could meet you, but why don't you come over, because we're not quite ready. . . . Yes, you're right, Fitzgerald is working on a song about a whale. . . . I think it's almost finished now, so why don't you hurry right along. . . . All right, we'll be looking for you. Good-bye."

Maggie hung up the receiver and turned back to her friends. "He's coming right over."

Fitzgerald got down from the piano stool and said, "Well, perhaps I'd better not sing until he comes. I'm sure he'll die if he doesn't hear my song."

Maggie laughed. "Oh, no he won't. He'll live very well without hearing your song, so sing it now and get it over with."

Fitzgerald, looking a little abused, climbed

21

back on the piano stool and, with a great sweep of his paws, began to sing:

> "*We are going to see nice Mr. Whale.*
> *He lives out in the ocean*
> *Where there's big waves and a gale,*
> *He's sure a great big fellow.*
> *He's bigger than a house,*
> *But he's not one bit smarter than*
> *His friend, who is a mouse.*"

Maggie Muggins picked up her sun hat and said, "All right, now you've sung your song, let's go."

"No, no, not yet," and Fitzgerald raised his paws over the piano keys again. His eyes were sparkling with fun as he went on. "There's a second verse, and I'm not going one step until I sing it."

Maggie sighed and put down her hat. The saucy little mouse sang again:

> "*The Whale's mouse friend has*
> *A very fine long tail,*
> *And some handsome whiskers.*
> *Though he's smaller than the whale,*
> *He's every bit as clever.*
> *He is a very smart mouse,*
> *And he wouldn't want to be*
> *As big as a whale or a house.*"

Fitzgerald swung around again and, winking at Petunia, said to Maggie, "Isn't that a lovely 'Whale' song, Maggie Muggins?"

Maggie couldn't help laughing, because the mouse had sung all about himself and not the whale. They were all laughing together as they left the little pink mouse house to meet Big Bite Beaver. The four of them turned toward the seashore. The breakers were pounding shoreward, and seemed to be calling a welcome to the little people.

Big Bite straightened his back, and Maggie climbed aboard. Petunia climbed to her knee, and Fitzgerald climbed into Petunia's cosy pocket and they were away. Big Bite's tail kept an even slap, slap, slap on the water as he carried his passengers to the deep sea home of the sea giant. They saw no sign of the big fellow, but suddenly Maggie cried out over the roar of the waves and the slapping of Big Bite's tail, "Big Bite, stop swimming for a minute. I thought I heard someone calling my name."

They all became very still, and cocked their ears to listen. Maggie had heard her name called because it came again. It was the unhappy voice of Mr. Whale coming from over yonder where the sun was shining.

"Mr. Whale," called Maggie in answer, "I'm

23

over here, with Fitzgerald and Petunia and Big Bite. Come and meet us, Mr. Whale."

"I can't move, Maggie," cried Mr. Whale. "Maggie, something has happened to me. I'm in trouble. I can't see what the trouble is because it's in my tail. Hurry, Maggie, please hurry. I'm hurt."

Big Bite's tail began to slap, slap the water with renewed vigour. The splashing waters fell over his passengers like a fountain, but they urged Big Bite on in spite of their discomfort.

Big Bite swam to a spot directly in front of Mr. Whale's great dark face. Maggie noticed that there were tears in his eyes, and she said softly, "Mr. Whale, what is it? What's the matter?"

"My tail. There's something sticking in it," the big fellow sobbed. "I don't know what it is, and my tail is so far away from my face that I can't see what it is that's sticking in me."

"Don't cry, Mr. Whale. We'll tell you in a minute what it is. We'll cruise around to the back of you and see what's there," said Maggie.

"Yes," said Fitzgerald, "We'll have you fixed up in no time, Mr. Whale. You're in good hands and paws now."

"Fitzgerald," Maggie whispered, "don't make any promises, in case we can't help him."

24

Big Bite then headed for the back of the whale, which was almost as far as going to the corner, because Mr. Whale was a very big Mr. Whale. When they reached his tail, Maggie cried out in alarm.

"My gracious, Aunt Matilda!" she said. "There certainly is something sticking in him. Look at it! What on earth can it be? It looks like a big sword."

Petunia 'possum nodded her head. Petunia knew that that was just what it was. A sword! "It done look like a sword, Honey Chil'," she said. " 'cause that what it be! That there thing what stick in poor Massy Whale am big sword belongin' to big swordfish. I done know how it get there too."

The other three waited anxiously for Petunia's explanation. "I done think big Mr. Swordfish swim he this way, bump he into Mr. Whale and snap, off come he sword and stick in Massy Whale."

Maggie nodded her head now. She knew that Petunia was right, and she said so. She called out to Mr. Whale that they had discovered what was hurting him. Mr. Whale sobbed loudly about his strange predicament and, through his tears, he asked Maggie if she would climb up on his back and pull the sword from his tail.

"Yes, three of us will climb aboard you, Mr. Whale. Big Bite will wait in the water. Hold still

fingers. He winked at Maggie, and then asked her a question.

"Maggie," he said, "how good a dentist do you think you could be?"

Maggie rolled her eyes and screwed up her little freckled face, and then said, "Oh, I think I could be a pretty good dentist if I had some pincers."

The little girl's face brightened like the sun after a shower. She understood. "I know why you asked me that, Mr. McGarrity. You're going to lend me your big pliers, and I'm going to pull out the sword, like a dentist pulls out a tooth."

"Exactly, Maggie. Do you think you can do it?"

"Of course I can do it," said Maggie. "Where are the pliers, sir?"

They were in the toolshed. In a few minutes Maggie was dashing again toward the seashore, knowing that in a little while Mr. Whale would be comfortable again. Big Bite was waiting for Maggie at the shoreline, and soon Maggie reached the waiting whale, and Fitzgerald and Petunia, who were on his broad back.

Maggie placed the pliers on the sword and said that when she cried "go" they were all to pull.

And then she called, "One, two, three, 'GO'."

Out came the sword and into the water with it tumbled the mouse. "Help, help," cried that little fellow. "Help, I'm in the water."

"Well, get out of it," said Maggie calmly. "You can, you know."

But, instead of getting out of the water, Fitzgerald climbed aboard the big sword and paddled around to the face of Mr. Whale so that he might see what had been the cause of all his unhappiness.

The big fellow thanked his little friends with all his big whale heart.

"We were glad to be of service, Mr. Whale," said Fitzgerald. "Any time you get a sword in your tail, just let us know."

A little while later Maggie was in the garden again. She told Mr. McGarrity that the pliers had worked, that the sword had come out and had tumbled into the water, along with Fitzgerald Fieldmouse.

"And, Mr. McGarrity," laughed the little girl, "that mouse started to scream for help. 'I'm in the water,' he said, but I just told him to get out of it because I knew he could get out easily. But, Mr. McGarrity, do you know what he did?"

"I'd never guess what that little fellow would do," laughed Mr. McGarrity.

"Then I'll tell you," said Maggie. "He climbed aboard the sword and paddled around to Mr. Whale's face so that Mr. Whale could see the sword that he'd had in his tail."

"I'm sure Mr. Whale must have been happy to see it," said Mr. McGarrity.

"He was," said Maggie. "He smiled. And if ever you want to see anything beautiful, Mr. McGarrity, just go and see a whale smile."

Mr. McGarrity bit his lip again as he answered, "I'll do that, Maggie. All in all, I'd say you'd had quite a day."

"Yes, sir," smiled Maggie Muggins, "because tra la, la la, la la, la lail, we pulled a sword out of Mr. Whale. I don't know what will happen tomorrow."

THE TOY HORSE

Maggie Muggins was dancing down the garden path. Her toes seemed to be full of twinkles that morning, and so did her eyes. She was very

31

happy as she made her way toward the garden singing,

"Tra la, la la, la la, la lee,
Here comes Maggie Muggins me,
I'm feeling so happy, tra la la ly
But I can't give you the reason why,
And, hello, Mr. McGarrity."

Mr. McGarrity smiled in his usual merry way at his little friend, and said in his usual merry way, "Hello yourself, Maggie Muggins, and what is this about being happy and not knowing why?"

"It's just like I said, sir," answered the little girl. "I'm happy and I don't know why. Mr. McGarrity, did you ever wake up of a morning feeling all sort of twinkly like the stars?"

"Yes, I have done that," said the old gardener. "I used to wake up feeling like that when I was a little shaver. But lately, when I wake up, I say to myself, 'Upon my red-handled hoe, I do wish I could stay in bed this morning'."

Maggie shook her head, and Maggie shook her finger at her friend. "Mr. McGarrity, you should never do that," she said, "and I'll tell you the because-why. If you stay in bed all you can see is the wall and the ceiling. But if you get up you can

32

see the sun and the birds, and the grass and the trees, and little dogs that run. There's things to see if you get up."

Mr. McGarrity agreed with Maggie, and went on to say, "Let's get back to this 'twinkly like the stars' feeling you have, Maggie. You don't suppose by any chance that you're going to get a present, do you?"

Maggie pondered over the idea for a minute, and then nodded her head. "Do you know, sir, I believe I am. I have sort of a 'presenty' feeling, too. Do you know the because-why of that, sir?"

Mr. McGarrity threw back his head now and roared with laughter. "Yes, I do," he said. "I do know the because-why of that. Of course I should make you guess about it, but I'll be kind."

Mr. McGarrity reached into the branches of the currant bush behind him, and brought out a little package, wrapped in the whitest of tissue paper. Maggie was so excited that she couldn't seem to break the string that was tied around it.

"Here, Butterfingers, give it to me," said Mr. McGarrity. He then unwrapped the parcel and Maggie gasped in delight at what he took out of the box. It was a toy horse.

"Oh, Mr. McGarrity, he's sweet, he's pretty,

he's darling, I love him and, do you know something? He's bigger than my friend Fitzgerald Fieldmouse."

"Well upon my red-handled hoe, he is, too. Fitzgerald can ride on him," said Mr. McGarrity.

"You mean 'pretend ride', don't you, sir?"

"I mean no such a thing," answered Mr. McGarrity. "This horse can gallop. He winds up. Let me show you."

There was a key in the side of the little toy horse, and in a few minutes he was galloping along the garden path at great speed. Maggie had to run to catch him before he bumped into the rose bush. She hugged his whirling little body to her as she returned to Mr. McGarrity.

"Look at him, sir, look, he's still galloping in the air. Oh, where on earth did you find such a lovely horse, Mr. McGarrity?"

"I was in town yesterday," said the old man, "and when I saw him in the shop window I thought to myself, 'Maggie Muggins would like that little horse', and so I bought him. By the way, his name is 'Whoa-there'."

"Whoa-there?" squealed Maggie. "Oh what a nice name for a little horse. Whoa there, Whoa-there!" But the little horse, whose key had not yet

34

stopped turning, kept right on galloping in Maggie's hands.

"He doesn't pay one bit of attention to me, Mr. McGarrity."

Mr. McGarrity laughed again. "He will when he runs down. Look, what did I tell you, his legs are getting slower . . . slower . . . slower . . . Whoa there, Whoa-there." The little horse became still. "You see, he obeyed me."

The two good friends laughed together all over again, and then Maggie thanked Mr. McGarrity and dashed off toward the meadow to show her treasure to her friend the fieldmouse, who lived in the little pink mouse house there. Maggie hoped that Petunia 'possum would be visiting Fitzgerald when she arrived. She got her wish. Petunia was in the cosy rocking chair near the window, and she waved a friendly paw at Maggie as the little girl ran up the front steps.

Maggie began to chant as she crossed the porch, "I've got a present, I've got a present. I've got a present."

Fitzgerald Fieldmouse mimicked her and danced up and down, also chanting, "Let's see the present, let's see the present, let's see the present!"

And then he stopped and leaned forward eagerly, saying "Is it for me, Maggie? Is the present for me?"

"It is not," said Maggie, grandly. "It's for me. Mr. McGarrity gave it to me. Look!" And Maggie produced the toy horse.

Fitzgerald squeaked excitedly as he cried, "Look, Petunia, look! It's a little horse." And he eyed the little horse suspiciously. "Is he alive, Maggie?"

"You know very well he isn't alive, Fitzgerald Fieldmouse. He's a toy. Isn't he sweet, Petunia?"

Mrs. 'possum, who had left her rocking chair to examine the little horse, smiled broadly and said, "Lan' sake, Honey Chil', I never did see prettier lil' toy horse in all of my born days."

"Neither did I," said Maggie. "And he'll go, too! You just have to wind this little key in his side and he'll go. His name is Whoa-there."

Fitzgerald turned a somersault and then said, "That sure is a funny name!" He bowed to the little horse most politely. "Hi there, Whoa-there!" Of course there was no answer, so the mouse turned up his nose and said, "Maggie, I think this is a very stupid nag. He didn't speak to me."

Maggie turned up her nose. "He's very particular. He doesn't speak to everybody!"

36

There was more laughter, and then the mouse suddenly leaped to the piano stool and, with a great flourish of paws, began to play, and then to sing,

"Maggie has a little horse
And the horse is very fine.
He's got a pretty little tail,
It's not as long and thin as mine,
But I like him just the same.
I'm going to climb up on his back
And while we're galloping up and down
His feet will go clack clack clack clack.
We'll ride across the meadow green,
And over pastures we shall go.
And then we'll come back home again
And I shall tell my horse to 'Whoa'. "

Maggie Muggins clapped her hands and Petunia 'possum clapped her paws, and they both told Fitzgerald that he was a very clever little mouse. He climbed down from the piano stool and bowed once more. Then he looked at Maggie with eager eyes that were full of hope, and he said, "I could ride him, you know, if somebody said I might ride him. I could ride that horse."

Maggie nodded her head. "I know you could

ride him.   Mr. McGarrity said that he was big enough for a mouse to ride."

Petunia looked at Fitzgerald and then at the toy horse and shook her head as if she didn't quite approve of the idea.   Maggie asked her what she was thinking.

"Well, lan' sake, Honey Chil', I jus' think to myself that that there lil' honey mouse mighty plump and fat.   He might 'bust' lil' horse.   That what I done thinkin'."

"I'd cry my eyes out if he broke my little horse," said Maggie, "but he won't, because Whoa-there is as strong as iron.   I know what to do!   We'll try him in the house first, before we go outdoors.   I'll wind him up just a little bit."   And Maggie gave the key three short twists, and Fitzgerald mounted the toy horse and was on his way across the room.

"Ride him, cowboy," squealed the little mouse, as Whoa-there galloped under the table.   "Ride him, cowboy."

Fitzgerald was becoming really excited when the little horse began to slow down. Then he stopped. Fitzgerald leaped from his back in disgust.   "He ran down, just when I was going to gallop under the piano."

Maggie laughed.   "I told you I was just going

to give him a little wind, but if I wind the key around, and around, and around, and around, he'll go right across the meadow and back. Come on, let's go out now and try him."

Excitedly the three friends left the house. Maggie was carrying the precious Whoa-there under her arm. They went well out into the meadow where it was clear and flat and bright. Maggie wound the horse again. This time she gave the key twenty-three long turns. The toy horse's legs were spinning when she set him on the ground, and she held him while the mouse mounted. When she released the horse he galloped away, carrying the squealing mouse. Maggie and Petunia cheered them on, screaming with laughter all the while.

Suddenly Maggie's face darkened, and she cried out in alarm, "Petunia, look, look! He's headed for the rock pile. Oh, my gracious Aunt Matilda, if Fitzgerald rides into that rock pile he'll break Whoa-there."

Petunia nodded her head wildly and screamed, "Hold your horses, Honey Mouse! Whoa there, Whoa-there!"

But Whoa-there wasn't stopping and, Maggie, seeing the great danger ahead, now screamed to Fitzgerald to turn the horse. Her advice came too late, because her answer was the sound of splintering wood.

Maggie burst into tears, and her sobbing echoed over the meadow and into the woodland. "He has broken my horse! He has broken him! Oh, you stupid mouse! You stupid, stupid mouse!"

Maggie broke into a run. Petunia was at her heels. When they reached the stone pile the little horse, that had been so gay and pretty a few minutes before, was now a heap of bits and pieces.

"Well, Fitzgerald Fieldmouse," cried Maggie to the mouse, although he was nowhere in sight, "I hope you're satisfied! My dear little horse is all broken to pieces! If you'd listened to me, and turned Whoa-there when I told you to, you wouldn't have bumped into the stone pile, but oh no, you . . ."

Maggie paused in her scolding. She realized now that the mouse was not there. She took it for granted that he must be in hiding. Still angry, she began to scold again. "I know you're there, some-where Fitzgerald Fieldmouse. You're hiding, and you may as well come out and 'take your medicine'. "

Petunia pulled at Maggie's pinafore, and Maggie looked down at Mrs. 'possum. "Honey Chil'," that lady said, "I don't think lil' mouse hiding."

"Then where is he?" asked Maggie.

Petunia shook her head fearfully. "Lan' sake, Honey Chil', I don't see hide nor hair of that lil' fellow. Here ussen is scolding he, and never once thinkin' what might have happened to he."

"What . . . what do you mean, Petunia?" asked Maggie Muggins very slowly.

"I mean I think we blame that lil' mouse for somethin' he don't do. I think that lil' horse run away with Honey Mouse. I don't think Fitzgerald could turn Whoa-there no how. And I think poor lil' mouse is all battered and bumped in middle of that rock pile."

"Oh, Petunia!" cried Maggie, as she climbed up on the rocks. "Come on, help me to look for him."

Together they searched every nook and cranny among the rocks and stones. They could not find him. Maggie was now crying in earnest. "And I was scolding him," she said to Mrs. 'possum. "I was blaming him, and it wasn't his fault. Oh, Petunia, where do you suppose he is?"

Petunia said that considering how the crash had been such a violent one, that the mouse might have been tossed into a tree top. Maggie called to a passing crow, "Mr. Crow, Mr. Crow, will you please look into the tree tops for us? Will you see if Fitzgerald Fieldmouse is up there?"

The crow, being a very obliging fellow, made a thorough search of all the trees in the vicinity, and cawed the bad news. "Naw, naw, naw," and went his way.

Maggie gulped in disappointment, "Petunia, if he's not in a tree, he must be in a cloud. Yes, I know he's been tossed into a cloud. You wait here and I'll go to Mr. McGarrity. He'll know how to get a mouse out of a cloud."

Maggie dashed toward the garden. She was not thinking of the splintered horse any more. She was thinking only of her little friend. She was positive now, in her own mind, that Fitzgerald was lost in the clouds. She ran into the garden calling out as she ran, "Mr. McGarrity, oh Mr. McGarrity, how shall I ever get him down?"

Mr. McGarrity looked quizzically at his little friend and said, "Get who down from where, Maggie?"

"Down from the clouds, sir!" And Maggie pointed skyward. "I think it's that one, sir. I think that's the cloud that was floating over the rock pile when it happened."

Mr. McGarrity shook his poor old head. Maggie did bring him such problems. "When what happened, Maggie?" he asked.

"The accident, sir. The accident!"

"WHAT accident, Maggie Muggins?"

"Whoa-there's accident! Don't you understand? He ran away. Fitzgerald was on his back when he ran away, and Whoa-there headed right for the stone pile, and 'bump' went Fitzgerald right over his head, and Whoa-there is a bunch of splinters and chips, and Fitzgerald is in a cloud, and please, Mr. McGarrity, how do I get him down?"

Mr. McGarrity leaned on his red-handled hoe and laughed until the branches of the currant bushes shook with his merriment. Maggie frowned in displeasure and said that she didn't think that it was funny to be tossed into a cloud.

"I don't think it's funny, either," said Mr. McGarrity, biting his lip to keep back further laughter, "but, Maggie Muggins, why do you say that Fitzgerald is in a cloud?"

"Well," said Maggie, "we couldn't find him in the rock pile, and Mr. Crow couldn't find him in the tree tops, so he must be in the clouds."

"Not necessarily," said the old man. "Now suppose you tell me just what happened before Fitzgerald went on his wild ride."

Maggie pondered. "Nothing much," she said thoughtfully. "I told Fitzgerald that he could ride

43

my horse, and Petunia was worried. Petunia said that Fitzgerald was fat and plump, and that he might break Whoa-there if he rode him, but I said I didn't think he would, but if he did, I'd cry my eyes out, and . . ."

"Stop right there, Maggie," said Mr. McGarrity.

"Yes, sir, I'm stopped," said Maggie, waiting anxiously for what Mr. McGarrity was going to say.

"You tell me," went on the old gardener, "that you told Fitzgerald that you'd cry your eyes out if anything happened to Whoa-there?"

Maggie nodded, and Mr. McGarrity smiled wisely. "I think," he said, "that when Fitzgerald did break the horse he remembered right away what you had said. And I think that that little mouse picked himself up and headed right into town to buy you another toy horse. Fitzgerald is a tender-hearted little fellow, and he didn't want to make you unhappy."

"Oh, Mr. McGarrity," said Maggie Muggins.

The old man picked up Maggie's two red pig-tails between his gnarled fingers and gently pulled her drooping head upward. He winked at her. "Now, now, no need to look so blue! Fitzgerald will forgive you for the scolding that he didn't hear. And

I think if you'll go back to his little pink mouse house now you'll find him there with another toy horse. Run along now, and see if I'm not right."

Maggie was smiling as she dashed again across the meadow to Fitzgerald's place. When she reached the pink mouse house she found a breathless little mouse, unwrapping a parcel. It was a toy horse.

"Fitzgerald," Maggie said. "Where have you been? We were so frightened!"

Fitzgerald, his tam o'shanter all awry, sobbed into his tiny handkerchief. "I . . . I broke Whoathere, Maggie. I didn't mean to break him. He ran away with me. But I was so sad. I didn't want you to 'cry your eyes out', Maggie, so I went to town to get another horse. Do you like him?"

"He's beautiful," said the little girl, looking at the new toy. "But I'm sorry you went to so much trouble. It was really an accident."

"I know," said Fitzgerald. "But just the same, I wanted you to have a horse. Here he is."

Maggie reached for the new horse and began to turn the key. "Do you want to ride him, Fitzgerald?"

Fitzgerald backed away. "No, thank you! I've had enough of horseback riding. I'm never going to drag a horse around with me again."

A laughing Maggie Muggins went back to the

45

garden to tell Mr. McGarrity that all was well again, and to show him the new horse.

"Upon my word," said Mr. McGarrity. "He is a beauty! Fitzgerald did try to make up to you for the accident, didn't he?"

"Yes, sir, and do you know something, Mr. McGarrity? I'm ashamed of Maggie Muggins for scolding and blaming. A person shouldn't scold other people when a thing is an accident, should a person?"

"No, a person shouldn't," agreed Mr. McGarrity. "All in all, Maggie, I'd say you'd had quite a day."

"Yes," smiled Maggie Muggins, "because tra la, la la, la la, la lorse, Fitzgerald went riding on a little toy horse. I don't know what will happen tomorrow."

THE STARFISH

A little red bird sang in the maple tree outside
Maggie Muggins' window. Maggie turned lazily in
bed, opened her blue eyes and laughed. "All right,
little Red Bird," she said. "I know it's another day.
I'll get up. Thank you for calling me."

47

Maggie Muggins got up and, almost before the Red Bird had finished his song, she was dancing down the garden path singing as happily as the Red Bird,

"Tra la, la la, la la, la lee
Here comes Maggie Muggins me,
And tra la, la la, la la, la lay
You don't know where I'm going today.
Do you, Mr. McGarrity, and 'hello'."

Her good friend in the garden leaned on his red-handled hoe and looked at his little hopping friend. He nodded his old grey head slowly and deliberately. "Hello yourself, Miss Muggins, and I do know where you're going today. What makes you think that I don't know?"

Maggie laughed. "Because I haven't told you where I'm going, so how could you know?"

"There are other ways of finding out things," said Mr. McGarrity. "I don't have to be told everything. And I happen to know where you're off to this morning, without being told."

"Tell me what you think, and I'll tell you if you're right," said the little girl, hopping on one foot around the currant bush.

"All right," said Mr. McGarrity, "I shall tell you. 'Tra la, la la, la la, la lee, Maggie's going to wade in

48

the sea, and tra la, la la, la la, la land, I think she'll build a castle of sand.' Now am I right or wrong?"

Maggie's blue eyes were dancing in time with her hopping feet. "You're right, sir, you're right, and I think you're wonderful. But how ever did you guess, Mr. McGarrity?"

"I didn't have to guess," said Mr. McGarrity. "I looked at you and I knew. First of all, you're wearing your old blue overalls. Second of all, you're in your bare feet and, third of all, you're carrying a lard kettle, which means that you're going to use it for a sand pail."

" 'Where I am going' was sticking out all over me, wasn't it, Mr. McGarrity?" said Maggie.

"It was indeed," laughed her friend. "And with whom are you going to build the sand castle, if I may ask?"

"With Fitzgerald Fieldmouse and Petunia 'possum, and anyone else who comes along. We don't mind who helps us to build the castle," said Maggie.

"I'm sure you'll have fun in the sand today," said Mr. McGarrity.

"So am I," smiled Maggie, "and now I think I'll take my bare feet over to the meadow. Good-bye, Mr. McGarrity."

"Good-bye, Maggie."

49

Maggie was away. The lard kettle was swinging back and forth at her side and it shone like a mirror as she danced past the scarlet runners, over the cabbage patch, under the hedge and off into the meadow. Petunia 'possum was at the little pink mouse house when Maggie arrived. Petunia was wearing an old lilac cotton dress and a straw hat. Fitzgerald was wearing overalls. They were rolled to his knees. Maggie laughed when she saw him.

"Fitzgerald," she said, "you look just like me, except that you haven't got red hair and freckles."

"And except that you haven't got whiskers and a long tail," laughed the little mouse. "Outside of those things we're the spittin' image of one another."

"Yes, aren't we, though?" said Maggie. And then she drew their attention to the lard kettle. "This is our sand pail. We may have to wet the sand, you know. I expect we'll make the biggest sand castle in the world."

Petunia nodded and Fitzgerald said, "We'll put turrets and towers on our castle, eh, Maggie? Just like the ones in the fairy tale books, eh, Maggie?"

"Yes," said Maggie, glowing with excitement. "It's just what we'll do. We'll build a fairy tale castle in the sand."

Petunia tied the strings on her straw hat tightly

under her chin and got up from the rocking chair. "Honey chillen," she said, "let us get for to go. I just can't wait to get my paws in that there sand."

"But Big Bite Beaver isn't here yet," said Maggie. "We can't leave without Big Bite. Where is he? Have you heard from him?"

Fitzgerald told Maggie that they had had a telephone call from Big Bite a little while previously, and at that time he said that he would be delayed. "And, in the meantime," said the mouse, "I'll sing a song for us, eh?"

Without waiting for an answer Fitzgerald seated himself at the piano and began to make up a song about the seashore. With great vigour he sang,

> *"We shall all go wading*
> *Out in the big deep blue sea.*
> *Maggie Muggins, Petunia, and Big Bite*
> *And little me.*
> *We're going to build a castle,*
> *And will it ever be nice.*
> *We'll make it big enough maybe*
> *To hold a little mice named Fitzgerald."*

Maggie laughed at the song and said, "That word in the last line should be 'Mouse', Fitzgerald."

"It should not . . . it should not," said Fitz-

51

gerald indignantly. "It should be 'mice'. 'Nice' and 'mouse' don't rhyme. If I'd put 'mouse' I'd have had to say the castle was 'nouse' and whoever heard tell of a 'nouse' castle."

"Oh all right, all right," said Maggie. "Don't get so excited about it."

Before Fitzgerald could further disagree with Maggie, Petunia announced that Big Bite Beaver was coming toward the pink mouse house, "An' Lan' sake," she cried, "is that honey beaver ever runnin'? He act as though there be somethin' after he."

Maggie joined Petunia at the window. "But no one is after him," she said. "He's alone. But he does look worried. Fitzgerald, he's almost here now. Open the door for him."

The little mouse swung the door wide and Big Bite, moving with more speed than his friends had ever seen him use before, came into the room and gasped, "My goodness! My goodness! My goodness!"

Maggie laughed. "All right, that's a 'my goodness' for each of us. Now please tell us what all these 'goodnesses' are for?"

Big Bite began his story. He told them that because he had been delayed, he feared that his friends might have gone on without him and so,

52

before coming to the mouse house he had gone to the shore to look for them. "And it was then I saw them!" he said. "It was then I saw them. Oh my goodness!"

Maggie took Big Bite by the shoulders and shook him. "Listen, Big Bite Beaver, I'll shake you good, if you don't tell us what you saw."

"The stars!" gasped Big Bite. "The stars! They've fallen out of the sky, Maggie. They're scattered all over the beach, and their lights are out."

Maggie laughed. "Big Bite Beaver, you've been seeing things," she said.

Big Bite nodded his head. "Yes, Maggie, I have been seeing things. I've been seeing the stars. They're all over on the beach, and there's not a twinkle in one of them."

Maggie's face darkened. She wrinkled her brows in thought. Big Bite was a truthful beaver. "But . . . but," she said anxiously, "it just can't be true."

"There's just one way to find out if it's true or not," said Fitzgerald, wisely, "and that's to go over to the beach and see for ourselves."

"I hope you've made a mistake, Big Bite," said Maggie, as she went across the porch with her three friends. They broke into a run when they reached the grassy bank near the shore. They hurried across the beach and headed for the shoreline. Big Bite pointed to the ground. Maggie cried out in alarm.

"Oh, Big Bite, you didn't make a mistake! The ground is covered with fallen stars, and there's not a light in any of them."

Fitzgerald had something to say about that. "They've likely broken their light bulbs when they fell. I knocked over my floor lamp once and broke the bulb in it. It's all very sad, Maggie, isn't it?"

"It's worse than 'sad', Fitzgerald. It's awful. The night sky will look so empty without the stars. What are we going to do? What can we do?"

Petunia, Big Bite, and Fitzgerald gave the question some thought. Then Fitzgerald suddenly flicked his tail and said, "I know what to do. I'll try to throw one of the stars back into the sky. If I could do that somebody up there would put a new bulb in it and it would light up again. And if I can get one into the sky, there's no reason why, between us, we couldn't get them all back in their places."

Maggie sighed, and said that the idea was worth a try. She advised Fitzgerald to begin with a little star. The little mouse picked up a little one, but the very instant he closed his fingers on it he gave a loud and painful squeal. "Owww . . . Owww . . . it's biting me." And he threw the star from him. It fell on a nearby rock and broke into several pieces.

"Fitzgerald," cried Maggie, "you've broken it."

"Well, serves it right," said the mouse, "it bit me."

"It didn't bite you!" said Maggie Muggins. "Stars don't bite. One of its points must have pricked you."

"I was bited!" said Fitzgerald. "Don't you think I don't know when I'm bited?"

Maggie corrected Fitzgerald for his use of the word 'bited', but before he could defend himself she went on to say that his idea of tossing the stars into the sky wouldn't work. "We'll break them all if we do that," she said, "and then we'll never have starry nights again. You wait here. I'll go to Mr. McGarrity. He'll know what to do."

Poor Mr. McGarrity! He did get so many strange problems to solve. But he was more amazed than usual when Maggie dashed into the garden saying, "The stars have fallen, sir, the stars have fallen."

Mr. McGarrity took off his straw hat, scratched his head, and put the hat back on again. "Well, upon my word, what is this you're saying?"

55

"I'm saying that the stars have fallen, sir, and I want to know how to get them back into the sky."

Mr. McGarrity laughed. "Now, Maggie Muggins," he said, "you're not trying to tell me that you've found some fallen stars."

"Yes, sir, I am trying to tell you that, and I'll tell you the because-why, too. We found the stars. The beach is covered with them. Big Bite Beaver found them first and he came and told us about them. We didn't believe either, but then we went with Big Bite to the shore and we saw them, and Mr. McGarrity, they're all out."

"Out?" said Mr. McGarrity, scratching his head again.

"Yes, sir, out! Their lights, I mean! They broke their bulbs when they fell, and not one of them is twinkling."

Mr. McGarrity roared with laughter now, and Maggie, half sobbingly said, "It's not very nice to laugh about it, Mr. McGarrity. How are you going to like it when there's never another starry night in the world."

"I'm not worrying," said the still laughing Mr. McGarrity.

"I wish I could say that," said Maggie. "We tried to do something about it. Fitzgerald tried to throw one little star back into the sky, but he squealed and said . . ."

"That it bit him?" asked Mr. McGarrity.

"Yes, sir. How did you know he said that? But he must have been wrong, because stars don't bite."

"But starfish do," said Mr. McGarrity, and he winked at Maggie Muggins.

Maggie began to laugh. "Starfish! They were starfish? And we thought . . . oh . . . oh, Mr. McGarrity." And Maggie's face filled with new alarm.

"What's the matter now, Maggie?" asked the old gardener.

"I told you that Fitzgerald threw one up into the air, didn't I? Well, when it bit him he threw it against the rocks and, Mr. McGarrity, it fell to pieces. That poor little starfish is . . . is . . . Oh, Mr. McGarrity, I can't bear to say it."

Mr. McGarrity patted the unhappy Maggie on her red head. "You don't need to say it, because the starfish is still alive. Everyone of those bits will become another starfish."

Maggie looked at Mr. McGarrity and said sadly, "You're just saying that to make me feel better, aren't you, Mr. McGarrity?"

"No, I'm not, Maggie. It's true. That's the way with starfish. The oyster fishermen discovered that a long time ago. Starfish eat oysters and they raid the oyster beds. The starfish can do what a man can't do, and that's to open an oyster with its fingers. It grips the shell of the oysters with its tiny suckers, and pulls. The oyster is a very strong fellow, but he's no match for the starfish. When the oyster fishermen first discovered this, they broke the starfish in the oyster beds into many pieces, and tossed the pieces back into the sea."

"And they found out that they were making more starfish to eat more of their oysters, eh?" said Maggie.

"Exactly," said Mr. McGarrity. "So you see now that Fitzgerald didn't really hurt the starfish at all."

"I'm glad," said Maggie, "because if it's one thing Fitzgerald doesn't want to do, it's to hurt another little creature."

Maggie ran back to the seashore then to tell her friends what she had learned. She found Fitzgerald sucking his sore finger.

"You didn't get bitten by a star after all, Fitzgerald," she said to the mouse.

58

Fitzgerald flushed angrily, "Maggie Muggins," he said, "do you think I don't know when I'm bited?"

" 'Bitten'," said Maggie.

" 'Bited'," said Fitzgerald. "If I want to be 'bited' I'll be 'bited', and I was 'bited'. "

Maggie laughed, "All right, you got 'bited', but not by a star, because these aren't stars, they're starfish."

"Well, my goodness!" gasped Big Bite Beaver, "No wonder there's no light bulbs in them then, eh?"

But no one answered Big Bite because they were looking at Fitzgerald. He'd suddenly burst into tears and was sobbing unrestrainedly into his little handkerchief. Maggie understood the reason for his grief, and she said, "Don't cry, Fitzgerald. You didn't hurt that starfish at all, when you broke him into pieces. There'll be a new starfish for every piece of him. Mr. McGarrity told me that, and Mr. McGarrity knows."

Maggie couldn't help laughing when she saw the astonishment on the faces of her little friends. And, leaving them wide-eyed and open-mouthed, she ran back to the garden to Mr. McGarrity.

"Oh, Mr. McGarrity," she said, "it was so funny to see their faces when I told them about the starfish. It is a very strange thing about them, isn't it, sir?"

"Yes, but there are many strange creatures in the sea. Did you know that there was a sea flower that ate fishes?"

Maggie shook her finger at Mr. McGarrity. "Now you are trying to make fun of me, sir. You don't expect me to believe that there's a flower that will eat a fish, do you?"

"Yes, I do. The sea anemone eats fish. It's a very beautiful flower, very gay in colour, and it eats fish."

"My gracious Aunt Matilda, what will you tell me next?" said Maggie.

"I'm going to tell you that, all in all, you've had quite a day."

"Yes, because tra la, la la, la la, la lars, we thought we'd found some fallen stars. I don't know what will happen tomorrow," said Maggie Muggins.

THE SOU'WESTER

The raindrops awakened Maggie Muggins that morning. "Drip drop, drip drop, drip drop," they said as they splashed, one after the other, against her window pane. Maggie laughed when she saw and heard the raindrops.

"You can't frighten me, little raindrops. You won't keep me in the house. I like you. I'm going to put on my raincoat, and go out and play with you."

Maggie Muggins was as good as her word. A little while later she was dancing down the garden path singing,

> "Tra la, la la, la la, la lain,
> Here comes Maggie in the rain.
> It's splishing, splashing lipperty
>   larrity,
> But where are you, Mr. McGarrity?"

Mr. McGarrity was not in the garden as usual, so Maggie cupped her hands and called through them, "Mr. McGarrity, where are you, sir?"

Her answer came from the toolshed. "I'm here, Maggie, in the toolshed. Come on in and see me."

Maggie, dripping with rain from head to toe, went into the toolshed where her friend was mending an old garden spade. She laughed as she said, "Are you scared of the raindrops, lipperty lea . . . why don't you come outdoors with me?"

Mr. McGarrity shook his old head. "No, I

won't go outdoors with you, Miss Muggins, and I am afraid of the raindrops—so lipperty led, I'm going to stay right here in the toolshed."

Maggie sighed, "It's really too bad, sir, because it's a beautiful day to wear a raincoat. I'm wearing mine, in case you didn't notice."

"I noticed," laughed Mr. McGarrity, "but I'm wondering where on earth you're going in your bare feet."

"Oh, you noticed that I was wearing my bare feet, too," said Maggie. "Well, that's because I don't want to get my good shoes wet and, besides, I like the feel of the rain splashing up and down between my toes. Rain will make my toes and your garden grow, did you know that, Mr. McGarrity?"

"I knew that," said Mr. McGarrity, "but it takes some sun with the rain to make both your toes and my garden grow. Did you know that?"

"Yes, sir," said Maggie. "We all need the rain and the sun, don't we? We're lucky to have them, aren't we? I guess I'm quite a lucky little girl to have a raincoat on a rainy day, because if I didn't have a raincoat my mother would probably say, 'Maggie, you can't go to the meadow today'."

"That's where you're off to, eh?" laughed Mr.

McGarrity. "Do you suppose Fitzgerald Fieldmouse will want to go out in a rain like this? He may prefer to stay home and read a good book."

Maggie howled with laughter at the idea of Fitzgerald wanting to stay home to read a book and, still laughing, she said good-bye to Mr. McGarrity, dashed out of the toolshed, across the cabbage patch, past the scarlet runners, under the hedge and off to the pink mouse house in the meadow. Maggie knew that Petunia 'possum would be waiting with the mouse. Both of her little friends liked rainy days as much as she did. Maggie's pigtails were dripping when she went into the little house. She shook them out and said, "Oh, my gracious Aunt Matilda, is the rain ever coming down."

"I know," agreed Fitzgerald. "It's pounding on my roof rat-a-tat-tat. I think that the rain thinks it's drumsticks and that my house is a drum. Sit down, Maggie."

"No, thank you," said Maggie. "If I sit down I may stay a while, and I don't want to do that. I want to get out into the rain again. The sun may come out any minute, and we'd miss splashing in the rain, eh, Petunia?"

Petunia shook her friendly head and laughed

as she said, "Lan' sake, Honey Chil', I don't done see how sun can come out pretty soon. Clouds hang low and heavy in sky."

Maggie sighed, "Even so, I don't think we should waste any time."

"It's not wasting time to sing," said Fitzgerald smugly, as he went to the piano stool and settled his music in front of him. Maggie glanced at the music and read its title, "The Rainy Day".

Fitzgerald looked into the little girl's face expectantly. She said nothing, and he asked, "Don't you want to hear my 'rainy day' song?"

Maggie laughed. "I'm going to hear it whether I want to or not, so I might as well sing with you," she said. "What is the tune of it?"

"It's the 'Polly Wolly Doodle' tune," Fitzgerald answered and, with great gusto, began to play.

The three of them sang,

> *"If there's one thing I like,*
> *It's a rainy day,*
> *'cause you can have so much fun*
> *when you play.*
> *You can run along the puddles*
> *And get up to your muddles,*

65

And sing along the way
Rainy day! Rainy day!
I sure like a rainy day,
No umbrella I'll be luggin'
When I go out with Maggie Muggin',
'cause all we'll do is laugh and play."

With the song over Maggie began to button her raincoat again. She noticed that Petunia looked a bit worried, and asked that lady what was the matter.

"I jus' thinkin' as I look out there, Honey Chil', that my pocket soon fill up if we walk in deep grass, and if it does I get so heavy I won't be able for to run."

"But we're not going to walk in the deep grass," said Maggie, "because if we did, we'd flatten it down so much that it wouldn't be able to stand up again and grow into hay. We're going to skip puddles in the gutters on the streets."

Fitzgerald burst into song again, singing,

"Here we come, skippy skoo,
Here we come, skippy skoo.
Over the puddles skip
Petunia and Maggie, me too."

66

"You're certainly full of singing today, Mr. Fieldmouse," said Maggie.

"I sure am," laughed Fitzgerald. "Well, let's go. I've got my raincoat and sou'wester on me, now."

Maggie turned to look at the little mouse, and cried out, "Oh Fitzgerald, where did you get the sweet little sou'wester? You look as cute as a button!"

Fitzgerald did look as cute as a button. The shining black sou'wester that he'd set jauntily on his head was hanging so low on his back that it almost reached his tail. He looked very pleased with himself. The merry little three left the house and made their way through the dripping weather to the gutters in a lonely lane. They knew better than to go to the main highway where the traffic was heavy. As soon as they reached the lane Maggie told them of a game that she had made up.

"It's called the 'puddle game', " she said. "Each one says a verse as he hops over a puddle. I'll do it first and show you what I mean." Maggie ran forward to a deep deep puddle, called out "Hippety hoppety slippety slump, over the puddle I now take a jump. Wheeeeeeee."

And she was over. Her little friends laughed and, understanding the game now, made ready to take turns. Petunia was second. She paused at the puddle's edge to make a verse. Her mind worked quickly, and she was ready, calling out her rhyme, "Lan' sake . . . I done lop, hippety hop, over the puddle, whippety whop . . . Wheeeeeee!"

And Petunia was over.

"It's your turn, Fitzgerald," laughed Maggie Muggins.

"I know, I know. Here I go," said Fitzgerald, making ready to spring. "Jumpety joo, lippety ly, over a puddle I hop and I fly . . . Wheeeeee."

The puddle game picked up speed now and, one after the other, they jumped over the puddles. Maggie had a new verse. "Look at me go, look at me hop. Over the puddle I'm now going to plop . . . Wheeeeeee."

And Petunia laughingly called out, "Watch I awhile . . . you Honey Chil', I hop over a puddle as wide as a mile . . . Wheeeeeeee."

And then it became very quiet behind Maggie and Petunia, and Maggie called out impatiently, "It's your turn, Fitzgerald. What's the matter, can't you make another verse, because if you can't, say so, and Petunia and I will keep on going."

There was no answer forthcoming from the

68

mouse. Maggie turned to Petunia, who was directly behind her, and said, "Petunia, would you please tell that mouse behind you to say his verse and hop his puddle."

Petunia looked behind her and, wide-eyed, turned back to Maggie. "Lan' sake, Honey Chil', there done be no mouse behind I. He not there any more. He gone."

"Not behind you?" said Maggie. "But he must be behind you."

Petunia shook her head. "I move out of line, Honey Chil', and you look for yourself."

Maggie looked. There was no sign of the mouse. Maggie called his name. Petunia called his name. And they both called together. There was still no answer. Together they retraced their steps and, when they turned the corner of the land, over the grating of a sewer hole lay the little sou'wester, alone. There was no mouse under it. Maggie cried out in alarm as she raced toward the lonely little hat.

"Petunia," gasped Maggie, "I know what has happened. He tried to hop over that sewer hole and he wasn't able to do it, and he was so small he fell through the grating. He must be down there. Petunia, put your eye to the grating and look down and see if you can see him."

69

Petunia fell to her knees and peered through the darkness below her. She saw nothing but the rushing waters that the rain storm had caused. She called and called, but no answer came.

All that was left of Fitzgerald Fieldmouse was the little sou'wester, and it couldn't talk. Maggie knew that there was nothing they could do now without help. She told Petunia to stand guard while she went to get that help from Mr. McGarrity.

Maggie flew to the toolshed. When she stood, dripping, before her old friend, who was still working on the garden spade, she said, "Mr. McGarrity, it's all my fault. I thought of it. I'm the one who thought of it."

Mr. McGarrity set down his spade and looked at the little girl. "You thought of what, Maggie? You told me that you were going to hop over puddles."

"I did. We did. We lipperty-lumped and jipperty-jumped, but it wasn't I who fell down into it. It was Fitzgerald."

Mr. McGarrity laughed as he said, "You mean Fitzgerald fell into a puddle?"

"No, but I wish he had," said Maggie.

Mr. McGarrity raised his eyebrows and said, "I

70

don't think it's very nice of you to wish that, Maggie."

"It would be better than falling into what he fell into," said Maggie. "It would be much better than that."

Mr. McGarrity said nothing. He waited for Maggie to get control of herself. She never got things straight for him when she was bouncing about in such an excited manner. When she finally calmed down, she began her story.

"It was like this, sir. Fitzgerald was wearing his sou'wester, that's how I know he's down there, because the sou'wester is on the grate. You see, we were hipperty-hopping in the gutter and we were each making up hopping songs, and then, all of a sudden, there was no song from Fitzgerald, and he was behind Petunia and Petunia was behind me."

"Yes, yes, go on. I understand so far. And then what?"

"Then we looked back, and Fitzgerald was gone and, Mr. McGarrity," sobbed Maggie, "his little sou-wester, his funny little sou'wester that looked so cute on him, was on the sewer grate, and he was gone."

71

"No," said Mr. McGarrity.

"Yes, and we called and called and he didn't answer," still sobbed Maggie, "because he wasn't down there."

"No, I'm not surprised at that," said Mr. McGarrity. "The rain is raining so hard that it's rushing through the sewers. I'll tell you what to do, Maggie, but you'll have to hurry."

"Yes, sir," said Maggie, anxiously.

"You take that fishing line in the corner there," said Mr. McGarrity. "It's got a hook on it. You and Petunia go to all the sewer grates further along the street. Call down through each grating. You'll catch up with him I know, if you hurry. He's being carried through the sewer pipes with the rushing water. He'll try to catch on to something to stop himself from being carried out to the river."

"Oh, Mr. McGarrity! But what's the fishing line for, sir?" asked Maggie.

"It's to fish Fitzgerald out of the sewer," said Mr. McGarrity. "When you hear him, drop the line and tell him to fasten the fish hook to his belt, and to hold on to the line with his paws. When he has done these things you can fish him out."

Maggie nodded. She was too unhappy and too

unsure about the whole thing to even thank Mr. McGarrity. But he knew that she was grateful for the help he had given.

She hurried to the waiting Petunia, told her of Mr. McGarrity's plan for Fitzgerald's rescue and, together, they raced along the gutters calling the little mouse's name at every grating in the street. At the eleventh one, the mouse answered.

"I'm down here, Maggie, I'm down here. I'm hanging on to a stick, but I'm swirling and swopping around and around. And, Maggie," he cried, "I've lost my sou'wester."

"Oh, for goodness sake," called Maggie in mock anger, "stop crying about the sou'wester. It's up here. We have it. Now listen to me. I'm going to drop a fishing line through the grating. You put the hook in your belt and then hold on to the line with your paws, and we'll fish you up."

Fitzgerald followed Maggie's instructions to the letter and, in a few minutes, he was back home and wearing the sou'wester. He would not take it off. Maggie shook her head as she said, "Fitzgerald, I just don't understand you. There you were, whirling about in that messy sewer, and all you were thinking about was a hat."

73

"But, Maggie," said the mouse, "it's the only sou'wester I have."

"It's the only life you have, too," said the little girl, "and you almost lost it."

Fitzgerald sighed deeply. "What would my life be worth without my sou'wester? That hat is my whole life," said the mouse.

Maggie raised her hands in despair, but she couldn't help laughing at the funny little fellow, who was really none the worse for his wild ride through the sewer pipes.

She was still laughing when she returned to the toolshed with the fishing line. Mr. McGarrity looked up from his work and said, "Well, the sun is shining again, I see."

Maggie looked through the window. "No, sir, it's still pouring rain," she said.

"Your face doesn't look as if it were. If I ever saw sunlight, it's on your face," smiled her old friend. "You saved Fitzgerald, I take it."

"Yes, sir," answered Maggie. "We saved him eleven sewer gratings down. And do you know something? When I called out to ask him if he were all right he said, 'Yes, but I've lost my sou'wester'. "

"No!"

"Yes, he said 'I've lost my sou'wester.' I told him that the sou'wester was safe, and I told him to fasten the hook to his belt, and he did, and we pulled him up."

"Good for you, Maggie," said Mr. McGarrity.

"Yes, sir," said Maggie. "And, do you know, Mr. McGarrity, I didn't know what a good fisherman I was at catching mice, until today. I caught him the first time I let down the line."

"I hope you advised Fitzgerald to take a warm bath and go to bed when you got him home," said Mr. McGarrity.

"Yes, sir, and he did, and he went, but he was wearing his sou'wester. Mr. McGarrity, he said that that sou'wester was his whole life. Of course he didn't mean it, but he sounded as if he did."

"Oh, he's quite a mouse. And, Maggie, all in all, I'd say that you'd had quite a day," said Mr. McGarrity.

"Yes, sir," agreed Maggie Muggins, "because tra la, la la, la la, la lating, poor Fitzgerald fell through the grating. I don't know what will happen tomorrow."

THE RED FIRE TRUCK

Maggie Muggins was braiding her red pigtails, when a pigeon flew through the branches of the maple tree outside her window, and dropped a little white note on the sill. Maggie picked it up, read it, and laughed, and in another few minutes was dancing

76

down the garden path toward Mr. McGarrity, with
the tiny letter tucked in her apron pocket.   She sang
as she danced,

> *Tra la, la la, la la, la lee,*
> *Here comes Maggie Muggins me,*
> *And I'm coming, tra la la lecret,*
> *Because I have a great big secret*
> *And hello, Mr. McGarrity, and wouldn't*
> *You like to know what my secret is?"*

"Hello, yourself, Maggie Muggins, and indeed
I would like to know your secret."

"So would I, sir," laughed the little girl.

"What's this, what's this?" asked Mr. McGarrity, leaning on his red-handled hoe.   "You say you
have a secret and then you say you'd like to know
what the secret is!   I don't understand."

"It is kind of mixy-up, isn't it, sir?" smiled
Maggie Muggins.

"It is very 'mixy-up', " laughed Mr. McGarrity.
"What is it all about, anyway?"

Maggie bit her lip and rolled her eyes as if she
were pondering the matter over, and then she shook
her head to show that she had not been successful in
deciding what it was all about.

"You see, Mr. McGarrity, it's like this. The secret isn't really my secret. It's Fitzgerald Fieldmouse's. He's the one that's got the secret."

And Maggie reached into the depths of her apron pocket, and brought out the little white note that the pigeon had brought to her earlier that morning.

"Read this, Mr. McGarrity," she said.

The old man reached into his overall pocket, got his spectacles, polished them with his red and white dotted handkerchief, put them on, and read:

> "*Dear Maggie:*
>
> *Hurry and get yourself out of bed and come over to my house. I've something red. You'll sure be surprised when you see what I've got. I'll say good-bye now, because I've got a lot of verses to make up for the song. I'm going to sing you about the something red. From your friend,* F. F."

Mr. McGarrity folded the tiny letter again, put his spectacles back into his pocket and said, "Well, upon my word! Now what do you suppose he's got over there?"

Maggie shook her head. "I don't know, sir. And, Mr. McGarrity, if I hadn't wanted to find out

78

I'd have climbed into bed again, because did you notice how cold it is this morning?"

"Yes, I have noticed," said the old man. "The shady side of the toolshed is still covered with heavy white frost. Did you notice that?"

"I didn't, but now I do, and look at the fence," said Maggie. "It's white too. But do you know something, Mr. McGarrity? Now that I am outdoors I'm glad because there's something about a frosty morning that makes me feel good and makes me run faster."

Mr. McGarrity laughed at Maggie's observations and agreed with her. "Not that I can run any faster," he said, "but I know you can, and if I were you I'd run as quickly as I could right now over to that pink mouse house in the meadow, to find out what this 'red something' is!"

"Yes, sir. I'll do that, sir," said Maggie, "because it must be something very mysterious, because if it wasn't Fitzgerald would never have sent Mrs. Pigeon over with that air mail letter."

"I don't suppose he would have," said Mr. McGarrity. "Off with you, and solve the mystery."

"Yes, sir," and Maggie suddenly shivered. "Brrrr," she laughed, "my nose feels red with the cold. Perhaps that's what Fitzgerald has, Mr. McGarrity, a red nose!"

And, leaving a laughing Mr. McGarrity behind her, Maggie dashed off through the frosty morning air to the little pink mouse house in the meadow. She found a very excited Petunia in the house with Fitzgerald. Old Grandmother Frog was there too. Maggie was astonished to see that old lady. Grandmother Frog was always complaining about her rheumatism, and so Maggie wondered at her coming out on such a frosty day. But there she was, and instead of complaining, she was giggling like a two-year-old. Maggie looked from one to the other. No one made any attempt to solve the mystery of the 'red something'. Maggie sighed. "Please don't be so mysterious. Tell me about it. I don't see anything red in the house."

Fitzgerald, his tiny black eyes brimming with mischief, said, "Do you know the 'because-why' of that? It isn't in the house."

Maggie was more puzzled than ever. "Won't somebody tell me?" And Maggie turned to Petunia 'possum. "You'll tell me, won't you, Petunia?"

Petunia looked at Fitzgerald and then back at Maggie. "Lan' sakes, Honey Chil', I like for to tell, but

80

I don't know whether I is supposed for to tell or not."

Maggie groaned in mock sorrow. She turned to Grandmother Frog. "Please, Grandmother Frog," she said, "you don't want to keep me waiting any longer, do you? Please tell me what it is, and where it is?"

The old frog cackled. "I . . . I guess there's no harm in telling you where it is. The 'red thing' is outdoors, back of the house."

Maggie ran through the living room and into the kitchen, but before she reached the window Fitzgerald called, "No, Maggie, no! Don't look. I want to tell you by song."

Maggie groaned again and, with lagging steps, returned to the living room and threw herself into a chair. "Fitzgerald," she said, "I could pull your tail."

Fitzgerald laughed. "I suppose you could, but you wouldn't, Maggie Muggins." He then swung around on the tiny piano stool and began his song.

> "*I have got a great big red surprise,*
> *You'll find it hard to believe your*
> *own two eyes.*
> *When you see what I have got outside*
> *Your big blue eyes will sure open wide.*"

The little mouse turned and looked at Maggie, a wide grin spreading across his face. Maggie made pretend to shake him, but he squealed, "Don't touch me, don't touch me. The second verse will tell you what it is."

"Well, sing it then," said Maggie. "Sing it."

Again Fitzgerald's paws fell on the keys, and the second verse began,

"I have got an engine for a fire an'
It has got a lovely big loud siren.
I can drive it all around about,
And I'll put all the mouse fires out
With my red fire engine."

Maggie squealed in excitement as she leaped to her feet again. "Oh, Fitzgerald, have you really got a red fire engine? Have you really?" But she didn't wait for his answer. She left her laughing friends and ran again to the kitchen and, this time, to the window. She looked out into the backyard beyond. There was a fire engine out there, but it was not red.

"Do you see it, Maggie?" called Fitzgerald from the living room. "Do you see the red fire truck?"

"I see a fire truck," answered Maggie, "but it's not red. It's white."

82

"It's red," said Fitzgerald. "Red's the colour of it."

"White's the colour of it," said Maggie.

"Maggie Muggins," said Fitzgerald coming into the kitchen, "you need spectacles. My fire truck is red."

Maggie moved away from the window. "Your fire truck is white. Come, look for yourself."

Fitzgerald looked out. He rubbed his eyes and looked again. He shook his head and looked a third time.

"Well," said Maggie smugly, "Do I need spectacles? Isn't that truck white?"

Fitzgerald nodded dumbly.

"You made a mistake, that's all," said Maggie. "You bought a white fire truck and thought it was red."

"I didn't! I didn't! I didn't!" cried Fitzgerald, jumping up and down in rage. "I drove a red fire truck into this yard, didn't I, Petunia?"

Petunia and Grandmother Frog, who had come into the kitchen when they heard the argument, both agreed with Fitzgerald. He had driven a red fire truck into the back yard.

"It was red like a honey apple when I see fire truck for first time," said Mrs. 'possum.

"Was it as red as an apple when you saw it, Grandmother Frog?" asked Maggie of the old lady.

"Well, well now, I . . . I thought it was," said the frog, "but of course I didn't sleep a wink all night (me rheumatism, you know) . . . so my eyesight may not be as good as it used to be."

Fitzgerald swung around and shook an angry paw in the old frog's face. "Your eyesight is every bit as good as it used to be, Grandmother Frog. You know very well that truck was red." And then his anger turned to sadness, and he half sobbed, "I know what has happened. Some wicked rascal has come along and painted the truck white. That's what happened."

"That's just what's happened," said Maggie, angry now too at this unknown person that Fitzgerald had just thought up. "We'll find the one who did it, too, and will I ever give him a piece of my 'Maggie Muggins' mind when we do find him. Come on, let's go. We have to find someone who is carrying a can of white paint."

Off set the angry four to make enquiries of their friends, near and far. Maggie said that she was sure that the 'white paint' person could not be very far away. They went to the pigpen first, to speak with

Grunter Pig.   They found Grunter rooting in the pen yard.

He greeted them in a very friendly manner, and listened attentively to their story, but he could not help them in their search.   He had seen no one with a can of white paint.

"But," he snorted, "Mr. Goat may have seen him.   Mr. Goat has been standing on the shed roof since sun-up.   Ask Mr. Goat, Maggie."

"Thank you, Grunter."   And a disappointed Maggie, followed by her three friends, went over to the shed and to Mr. Goat. She asked the all-important question.

"Mr. Goat, have you seen anyone passing this way, carrying a can of white paint?"

"Naaa, Naaa," bleated Mr. Goat.   "I have been standing here since the sun came up and I've seen no one with white paint."

After making several more enquiries here and there and around and about, Maggie sighed.   "It's just no use.   They've just not noticed the villain, that's all.   I'll go to Mr. McGarrity.   He uses his eyes."

Mr. McGarrity stopped his work when he saw Maggie running toward him, and he leaned on his red-handled hoe to wait for her.   He knew that

Maggie was in some sort of trouble, but before he could ask her what it was, Maggie cried out to him, "Mr. McGarrity, did you see him, did he go this way?"

"I don't know," smiled Mr. McGarrity, "whether I've seen him or not. Whom was I supposed to see?"

"You weren't supposed to see him, exactly, but I was hoping you did. Did you?" asked Maggie.

"Just a minute, Miss Muggins," said her friend in the garden. "I don't know what you're talking about. Just calm down, and tell me whom you hoped I'd seen."

"The one with the white paint," said Maggie. "Did you see anyone going by here with a can of white paint?"

Mr. McGarrity shook his head, and said, "No, did you lose a can of white paint, Maggie?"

"No, sir, but . . ."

"If you need some white paint, I think there's some in the toolshed," said Mr. McGarrity.

"Mr. McGarrity," cried Maggie "you don't understand. Will you please listen to me."

Mr. McGarrity said that he would listen, so Maggie began her story. "You know the little white note that Fitzgerald sent me?"

"Yes, the note in which he told you about something red? I remember," said Mr. McGarrity.

"The something red was a red fire truck, Mr. McGarrity, except that it's white," said Maggie.

"Dear me, dear me," said the old man. "What ever made Fitzgerald get a white fire truck. Fire trucks are always red."

"I know they are, Mr. McGarrity," said Maggie, trying her best to be patient. "Fitzgerald got a red truck, and he brought a red truck home, and he put it out behind his house, and he sang a song about a red truck, but when I went to look at it, it was white."

"No," said Mr. McGarrity.

"Yes, white! And, Mr. McGarrity, we know it was someone who was jealous of Fitzgerald for having a red fire truck (Fitzgerald was going to put out mouse fires with it, you know), and we think that jealous someone came along and painted the red truck white, and we're looking for someone with a can of white paint, and have you seen him?"

Mr. McGarrity didn't answer. He couldn't answer because he was laughing too merrily. Maggie looked very unhappy as she said, "It isn't funny, sir, it's sad."

"I don't think so, Maggie," said the old man.

87

"And, after we talk this situation over, you won't think it sad, either. Now, to begin. You said that Fitzgerald's fire truck was at the back of the house?"

"Yes, sir."

"Was the sun shining on the front or the back of the house?" went on Mr. McGarrity.

Maggie answered promptly. "At the front, sir. I remember it was shining in over the porch. But I'm not talking about the sun. I'm talking about the fire truck, and the villain who painted it white."

"So am I, Maggie, so am I," said Mr. McGarrity.

"You mean that you know him?" asked Maggie.

"I think so," smiled Mr. McGarrity. "Maggie, did you feel the white paint with your fingers, or did you just look at it?"

"I just looked at it through the kitchen window. We were in too much of a hurry to catch the villain to stop to feel the paint," answered the anxious Maggie Muggins.

Mr. McGarrity winked at the little girl. "I'm afraid you've undertaken quite a job. You'll never be able to catch the villain who painted the truck. Do you think you could catch the villain who painted the toolshed roof white?"

"But the toolshed roof isn't painted. That's

frost on the toolshed." And then Maggie burst out laughing. "Oh, Mr. McGarrity, the red truck isn't white, it's frosted."

"Exactly," said Maggie's good friend. "I'll tell you what to do, Maggie. You go over to the pink mouse house again, get into that truck and drive it into the sun. Fitzgerald will soon have a red truck again."

"Yes, sir, I'll do it." Maggie looked up at her friend. "Mr. McGarrity, I suppose you're ashamed of me for being so stupid."

"A little bit," said Mr. McGarrity.

Maggie was blushing as she ran back to the meadow. She didn't say a word to her waiting friends. She ran to the back of the house, got into the fire truck and drove it around to the front of the house. Fitzgerald, Petunia, and Grandmother Frog stood silently by waiting to hear what she had learned from Mr. McGarrity. From her seat in the truck she called out to the expectant three.

"Watch me," she said. "I'm going to work magic. 'White paint melt away and leave a red truck here today.' "

The sun, pouring down its warm rays, worked the magic for Maggie. The frost turned to water and trickled to the ground.

Fitzgerald was the first to understand what had happened. He began to wave his tam o'shanter wildly. "It was frost! It wasn't white paint, it was frost."

"Yes," laughed Maggie, "and Jack Frost was the villain that we were searching for."

They all laughed merrily together at their stupidity, and then Maggie went back to the garden.

Mr. McGarrity smiled as he looked into Maggie Muggins' twinkling eyes. "Fitzgerald Fieldmouse has a red fire truck again, eh?" he said.

"Yes, sir, and you should have seen my friends' faces when it began to turn red. I played I was making magic, and I said magic words, and the sun did the rest. Fitzgerald was the first one to know what had happened. He jumped around waving his green tam o'shanter, and he squealed, 'It's not white paint, it's frost!' And then we all talked about how stupid we had been, and then I came back here to you."

"Well, Maggie, it would seem to me that, all in all, you've had quite a day," said Mr. McGarrity.

"Yes, sir," laughed Maggie, "because tra la, la la, la la lost, Fitzgerald's red truck was painted with frost. I don't know what will happen tomorrow."

KITTEN-CATCH

A little sunbeam slipped through the branches
of the maple tree and kissed a sleeping Maggie
Muggins on the nose. Maggie tried to brush the mischievous sunbeam away, but the sunbeam danced

merrily and kissed her again. Maggie opened her eyes, laughed when she saw the golden rascal, and made ready to greet another day.

As she was hopping down the garden path toward Mr. McGarrity, she sang in her usual way,

> *"Tra la, la la, la la, la luggins*
> *Here comes Maggie, Maggie Muggins.*
> *I'm coming, tra la, la lo*
> *Just to say 'hello, hello' to Mr.*
> *McGarrity.*
> *Hello, Mr. McGarrity."*

Mr. McGarrity waved his straw hat at the oncoming little girl and said in his usual way, "Hello, yourself, Maggie Muggins, and how are you today?"

"I'm feeling fine outside," said Maggie, "but inside, I'm a puzzle."

Mr. McGarrity laughed. "What makes you a puzzle inside, Maggie?" he asked.

"It's because I don't know what to do today. That's what makes me a puzzle. A little sunbeam kissed my nose and woke me up, and the minute my eyes were open I said to myself, 'Maggie Muggins, what are you going to do today?' And do you know what I answered me, Mr. McGarrity?"

92

"No, I don't know," said her old friend.

"You're right," said Maggie. "That's just what I said. 'I don't know.' Mr. McGarrity, do you know what would be fun for a little girl named Maggie Muggins, a little mouse named Fitzgerald Field-mouse, and a little 'possum named Petunia?"

Mr. McGarrity looked at Maggie in astonishment and said, "Maggie, your question surprises me. You shouldn't have to ask anyone what to do on a nice day like this. There are so many things to do and see in this wonderful world of ours."

Maggie Muggins sighed, and looked up at the old man in a most angelic way. "I know, sir, but I've seen everything, and I've done everything."

Mr. McGarrity laughed again. "Have you now?"

"Yes, sir," said Maggie.

"Maggie Muggins!" said Mr. McGarrity, reprovingly.

"Well," said Maggie a little more slowly, "almost everything."

"Maggie!" chided the old man.

Maggie sighed again as she said, "I suppose there may be a few things that I have not seen and done. But I've heard everything." And she screwed up her

93

little freckled face as if she were challenging Mr. McGarrity, as she went on to say, "Tell me something that I haven't heard."

Mr. McGarrity smiled and said, "All right, I shall. You haven't heard the song I'm going to sing, because I'm going to make it up and so no one, up to now, has heard it." And Mr. McGarrity, threw back his merry old head and sang,

"Maggie Muggins is my friend.
She has a bright red head,
But she's not using it today.
I know that, 'cause she said
That she had seen just everything
In this great big wide world,
And that makes her a silly child,
A very silly girl."

Maggie nodded and said, "Yes, it does, doesn't it? I am a silly child, just as the song that you made up said. Mr. McGarrity, do you know something? I'm going to make up something too. I'm going to make up a brand new game, and I'm going to play it with Petunia and Fitzgerald and Newcome Kitten. I've not seen that kitten for a long time. He's been so lazy lately."

"I've noticed that," said Mr. McGarrity. "He lies in the sun all the time."

"He's sunning himself," said Maggie. "But I'm not going to let him do that today. I'm going to call him up when I get over to Fitzgerald's house. He'll have fun if he plays with us."

"I'm sure he will," agreed Mr. McGarrity. "And now that you've got plans for today, why don't you run off and get your games started."

"That's just what I'll do. Good-bye, sir."

Maggie Muggins ran off to the little pink mouse house in the meadow. Fitzgerald and Petunia were waiting for her. They always looked forward to Maggie's visits because, when Maggie was with them, there was always fun and adventure. As the little girl entered the house she greeted them gaily.

"Good day to you, Fitzgerald Fieldmouse, and good day to you, Mrs. 'possum."

Fitzgerald bowed and returned her greeting and Petunia, laughing, told Maggie Muggins that she was sitting "on top of the happy ol' world".

"I am, too," said Maggie Muggins. "I'm sitting on top of the world, too."

"I'd better climb up there with you," laughed

95

the little mouse. "I seem to be the only one with my feet on the ground."

Maggie made pretend that she was pulling Fitzgerald up to the top of the world, and he made pretend that he was puffing with the hard climb. And then he cried out, "Oh, look! Look down there at all the people and automobiles and things."

They all laughed together because they were acting silly, and then Maggie held up her hand. "Listen to me," she said, "we've done enough pretending. Let's get our feet on the ground again. I'm going to jump off at the top of the world and call up Newcome Kitten. Let's make up a funny game to play when he comes over."

"Yes, let's," said Fitzgerald. "And, because we haven't seen Newcome for a long time, let's make a 'Kitten Game'. "

"A game like 'CATCH', perhaps?" suggested Maggie.

"Yes," squealed Fitzgerald. " 'CATCH' has a 'cat' in it. So that makes it a kitten game, doesn't it?"

"Yes," laughed Maggie Muggins. "We'll call our game 'Kitten-Catch'. "

Petunia thought that a very clever idea, and praised her two friends for thinking of it. Fitzgerald

̄eaped to the piano stool. "I'm going to make a 'Kitten-Catch' song," he said. "I'll make words for the 'Looby Loo' tune. Everybody knows that game song."

After a few seconds of thought Fitzgerald had his first verse finished, and he sang,

> *"Now we play kitten-catch,*
> *Now we play kitten-catch,*
> *Now we play kitten-catch,*
> *Out in the strawberry patch.*
> *We put our right paw out,*
> *We put out left paw in,*
> *We flick our long and our hand-*
> *   some tails,*
> *And turn ourselves about."*

Maggie applauded loudly and urged Fitzgerald to compose a second verse. "And while you're doing it, Fitzgerald, I'll call Newcome."

Maggie went to the tiny telephone and dialled the kitten's home telephone number. Newcome did not answer the telephone himself. Maggie asked to speak to him. While she was waiting for him to come to speak with her she turned to her friends and said, "That lazy kitten is sunning himself again today. Oh, excuse me, here he is now. Hello . . . hello, is

97

that you, Newcome? . . . Yes, it is a long time since we've seen you. Newcome, we'd like you to come over and play with us. . . . Oh, I'm glad that you will. . . . And, do you know something, Newcome? We've made up a game just for you. . . . Yes, I think it was nice of us. It's called 'kitten-catch.' . . . All right, you hurry right over. Good-bye."

Maggie hung up the receiver and went to help Fitzgerald with the second verse of the 'kitten-catch' song. It was finished in no time and, as Newcome had not yet arrived, they began a third, and then a fourth verse.

Maggie looked at the clock. More than an hour had passed and Newcome had still not shown himself. Maggie became worried. She suggested then that they go meet the tardy kitten. They crossed the meadow, but there was no sign of him anywhere around or about. When they reached the barnyard Maggie saw Grunter Pig, and she went to him. "Grunter, we're looking for Newcome Kitten. Have you seen him?"

"No," snorted Grunter, "I didn't see him. But I did hear him mieowing a little while ago."

Maggie looked puzzled. "You heard him mieowing? Grunter, what kind of a mieow was it?"

"At first it was happy," said the friendly pig, "and then it was sad. And then I didn't hear any more mieowing. I heard someone pounding."

Then they all heard pounding. It sounded as if someone were knocking a tin can against the ground. The knocking was followed by a sad wail and cry for help.

"He's over that way," said Maggie, as she pointed beyond the pigpen. "And he's in trouble. Come on."

They all ran in the direction of the sound and, to their dismay, they found Newcome Kitten with his head inside of a salmon can. He was threshing about this way and that, and pounding the can on the ground. He was mieowing painfully and unhappily.

Maggie cried out to him. "Don't do that, Newcome. Stand still. You're making it all the worse by jumping around."

The kitten, who could not see Maggie, cried out through his tin mask, "Help me, Maggie. Get me out of here, please, and hurry."

"I'll try," said Maggie, "but it's not going to be very easy, because the can has jagged edges. Oh, Newcome, how did you get into that salmon tin, anyway?"

"Lan' sake, Honey Chil'," said Petunia 'possum,

"don't ask questions now. Just hurry and get poor little Honey Kitten outen that there tin."

Maggie took hold of the salmon tin and pulled. Newcome screamed in pain. Maggie sighed unhappily. "I told you, Newcome, I told you it would hurt. Oh, dear, what can we do?"

Maggie pondered and then her face brightened. "I know," she said, turning to the little mouse. "Fitzgerald, you squeeze into the tin."

"Who, me?" gasped Fitzgerald.

"Yes, you," said Maggie. "I can't get into a salmon tin, and neither can Petunia."

"But what's the sense of my getting into that tin can? One's enough," said Fitzgerald. "I don't see any sense in it at all."

"There's quite a lot of sense," said Maggie. "If you go in there you can gnaw the tin away and make a bigger hole in the can, and then Newcome can get his head out."

"But, but . . . but," stammered the little mouse, "there's no room for me to get into the salmon can."

"There will be if Newcome takes a deep breath. If he breathes in and holds his breath, you'll be able to squeeze in under his chin. I've seen you getting through smaller holes than that. And once you're in the tin, you can gnaw."

100

Fitzgerald bit his lip and sighed, and then gave in. "All right," he said, "I'll go. But I don't like it. Breathe in, Newcome."

"Yes, breathe in, Newcome. Pull in a big deep breath and hold it," said Maggie.

The frenzied kitten did as he was bade, and Fitzgerald, swift of movement, managed to get into the salmon tin. Once inside the vessel, the little mouse began to scream. "Help, help. Get me out of here. I can't get my teeth into the tin, and besides that, the jagged edges are hurting me and it's dark, too, and fishy. Let me out! Get me out!" And Fitzgerald began to pound frantically on the side of the tin, and Newcome Kitten began to cry.

"Oh, my gracious Aunt Matilda," said Maggie. "Be quiet, Fitzgerald. We'll let you out. Newcome, take another deep breath so that he can get out."

But Newcome paid no attention to Maggie's request. He was crying so loudly over the fact that Fitzgerald could not gnaw the tin that he paid no heed to anyone. He began to pound his tin-covered head on the ground again, mieowing all the while. Fitzgerald was screaming all the while, and begging to be freed. The whole thing was too much for Maggie Muggins. She left the mieowing kitten, the

101

squealing mouse, and the bewildered 'possum, and went racing to the garden to Mr. McGarrity.

She cried out as she reached him. "Now there's two of them in it, Mr. McGarrity. Now there's two of them in it! And it's all my fault."

"Two of them in what? And what's your fault, Maggie?" asked Mr. McGarrity as he leaned on his red-handled hoe to listen.

"It's my fault that they're in it, because if I hadn't asked him over to play 'kitten-catch' he'd still be in the sun, sunning himself. But I asked him to play 'kitten-catch' and now he's in it. And so is Fitzgerald, and that's my fault too, because I told Fitzgerald to go into it and gnaw, and he can't gnaw it, and what'll I do, Mr. McGarrity?" cried Maggie breathlessly.

"I have no idea what you'll do," said Mr. McGarrity calmly.

Maggie almost screamed her disappointment. "But, Mr. McGarrity, you've got to help me, sir. You've just got to help me to get them out."

"I might be able to do that if you'd just tell me what this is all about. I'm completely in the dark as to who is in where," said the old man.

"Oh," cried Maggie, "I forgot to tell you, didn't I?"

102

"You did," said Mr. McGarrity.

"It's Newcome," said Maggie. "He's in a salmon can . . . that is, his head is in a salmon tin. He was coming over to play 'kitten-catch', and on his way he met a salmon can."

Mr. McGarrity laughed at that. He couldn't help it, but he managed to say, "Go on, Maggie, go on."

"Yes, sir. He put his head into the salmon tin to lap up the little specks of salmon, and he got caught in there, and he banged his head around on the ground, and that only made it worse, and when we found him I told him to keep still."

"That was good advice," approved Mr. McGarrity.

"I thought so, sir, and then I told Fitzgerald that he'd have to squeeze into the salmon can and gnaw a bigger hole so that Newcome could get out. He didn't want to go at all, Mr. McGarrity, but I told him that it was the only way to help the kitten, so the poor little fellow squeezed in, but he couldn't get his teeth into the tin, and now Newcome is banging around again and, oh dear!" And Maggie, weary from her long breathless story, leaned against Mr. McGarrity's blue overalls and cried.

"There, there now, Maggie," said Mr. McGar-

103

rity kindly, as he stroked her red head. "Just calm down. I can help you."

Maggie looked up hopefully.

"I'm going to ask you a question, Maggie," said Mr. McGarrity. "How does your mother get salmon out of a tin?"

"She uses the can-opener." And a light, almost as bright as the little sunbeam that had kissed Maggie earlier, spread across her face.

"Mr. McGarrity, thank you," said the little girl. And she ran toward her own home, and the kitchen. Quickly she seized the can-opener from its place in the table drawer and, like a flash, she made her way back to her friends.

Newcome was still threshing about. Fitzgerald was still squealing, and Petunia was still standing by, in a very bewildered state. Maggie caught the kitten and, with deft hands, used the can-opener to free him from his tin prison.

Of course Fitzgerald was freed at the same time, and he was inclined to be indignant. "Maggie Muggins," he cried, "the next time you can me, I'll . . . I'll . . ."

In the middle of Fitzgerald's tirade he burst out laughing. "Say, Maggie," he said, "can you smell me? I'm fishy."

Maggie sniffed. "You certainly are," she said. "So is Newcome. It's a bath for both of you! Hurry off now and bathe. Then we'll play 'kitten-catch'. "

A while later, when they had wearied of the game, Maggie made her way back to the garden.

"You're looking so pleased with yourself, Miss Muggins, that I presume the can-opener did its work?" said Mr. McGarrity.

"Yes, sir, it did its work well. I had quite a time catching that kitten. He was still banging around with poor Fitzgerald when I went back, but I did catch him, and I got them both out of the tin. Fitzgerald was going to be angry at me but he changed his mind, and do you know why?"

Mr. McGarrity shook his head.

"He began to laugh, and you can't be angry when you laugh, and he was laughing because he smelled like a salmon. I made both Newcome and Fitzgerald take a bath. After they were cleaned up we played 'kitten-catch' and had fun."

"Good! I'm glad to hear it. All in all, Maggie, you've had quite a day," said Mr. McGarrity.

"Yes, sir, because tra la, la la, la la, la lan, Newcome got caught in a salmon can. I don't know what I'll do tomorrow," said Maggie Muggins.

HIS MAJESTY'S TEA PARTY

Maggie Muggins was very excited that morning. She had found a letter on her window sill, and the letter, which was from her little friend Fitzgerald Fieldmouse, had a very mysterious air about it.

106

Maggie loved mysteries, and so she was singing as she danced down the garden path.

> " *Tra la, la la, la la, la luggins,*
> *Here comes Maggie, Maggie Muggins.*
> *I'm going some place, tra la la lare,*
> *Ask me, ask me, ask me where.*
> *I'm going, Mr. McGarrity, and*
> *'hello'.* "

Mr. McGarrity, being both obliging and curious, did ask Maggie where she was going. But he was astonished by her answer.

"I don't know, sir," said Maggie. "I don't know where I'm going."

Mr. McGarrity was perplexed. "Maggie," he said, "I'm a bit muddled. You tell me to ask you where you're going. I do that, and then you tell me that you don't know yourself."

"And I don't, sir, but if you think back a little minute you'll remember that I didn't once tell you that I knew where I was going," said Maggie.

Mr. McGarrity thought back the little minute and agreed with Maggie that she had not once said that she knew where she was going.

"But you must have some idea of what you're talking about," said her old friend. "I hope you do, because I haven't."

Maggie laughed, and handed Mr. McGarrity the note she had found on her window sill. "Have you got your spectacles with you, because you'll need them. The writing is very small. It's mouse-writing."

Mr. McGarrity laughed now as he reached into his pocket for his spectacles. He put them on and read,

> "*Dear Maggie Muggins:*
>   *Hurry over*
>   *Through the grass and through the clover.*
>   *We're going some place, you and me*
>   *And Petunia, and we'll see*
>   *Someone that we have not saw*
>   *For a long time, tra la la.*   F. F."

"The 'F. F.' stands for 'Fitzgerald Fieldmouse'. He always signs his letters with his initials. Mine are 'M. M.', " said Maggie Muggins.

"Thank you for telling me," laughed the old man, "but, Maggie, will you tell that little mouse that I don't think much of his letter. He should have said, 'you and I', and he should have said 'have not seen'. "

108

"But he was writing poetry," said Maggie, defending her little friend. "And, besides that, sir, he's such a little mouse."

"Being small is no excuse," said Mr. McGarrity. "It's when you are small that you should learn to talk properly."

Maggie nodded her head and said, "I try to talk properly, sir. Of course, there are times when I make up a few words of my own."

"Yes, you have quite a few words of your own, Miss Muggins, but I know that you make them up just for fun," smiled her friend.

"Yes, sir, they're just for fun. I hope I have fun at the mysterious party, don't you, Mr. McGarrity?" asked the little girl.

"I do, indeed," answered Mr. McGarrity. "And when you find out what the mystery is all about, come back and tell me."

"Yes, sir, and now I think I should go. They'll be waiting for me. Good-bye, Mr. McGarrity."

"Good-bye, Maggie," said Mr. McGarrity. And he watched her as she ran across the cabbage patch, past the scarlet runners, under the hedge and off to the meadow.

Maggie was wondering as she ran what excitement lay ahead. She found Petunia 'possum and Grandmother Frog at the little pink mouse house with the mouse when she arrived. Maggie didn't wait for the usual polite greetings. She burst into the house saying, "Tell me, Fitzgerald, tell me where we're going?"

The mouse laughed and said, "Did you 'hurry over through the grass and clover', Maggie?"

"Yes, I did and, Fitzgerald, don't be a 'meany'. Please tell me what you meant in your letter."

But Fitzgerald had made up his mind to make this mystery last as long as possible, and announced to his guests that he would reveal all through a song.

"Oh dear," said Maggie, stamping her foot impatiently, "that's the slow way, isn't it, Petunia?"

Petunia nodded. "It sho' nuff is, Honey Chil', but I done guess it only way ussen goin' for to fin' out."

Maggie raised her eyebrows and looked from Petunia to Grandmother Frog. "Then you two don't know what it's all about, either?"

Grandmother Frog shook her old head. "No, no, we don't know, Maggie. I found a letter from Fitzgerald on my lily pad this morning. I got up just as the mailman was coming along. Of course I could have been up hours earlier. I didn't sleep a wink all night."

"I know," said Maggie, "it was your rheumatism that kept you awake." Maggie smiled mischievously. "But you felt well enough to come over here this morning, didn't you, Grandmother Frog?"

"Well . . . I . . . I . . . well now, it was like this," stammered the old frog. "I thought that the mystery would take me mind off me rheumatism . . . yes, yes, . . . that's what I thought."

"And it will, too," said Maggie, "if we ever find out what it's all about."

With a smug flick of his tail, Fitzgerald went to the tiny piano, and he sang,

> "*Just this morning,*
> *Guess whom I did see*
> *When I was out for a morning stroll.*
> *Guess who did call to me,*
> *Our little friend the seahorse.*
> *Gittyep is his name.*
> *He saw me and he laughed, and then*
> *Out of the sea he came.*"

Fitzgerald swirled around on the piano stool and looked at his expectant friends. There was silence for a few seconds, and then Maggie said, "Well, what of it? He came out of the sea! But something else must have happened."

Petunia nodded her head and said, "Yes, Honey Mouse, something else must have happened. There's nothin' in that there song of yours to get ussen excited. The honey seahorse often comes out of sea."

Maggie got up from her chair and went toward Fitzgerald with clutched hands. "Fitzgerald," she said, "there's a second verse to that song, and if you don't sing it this very minute I'm going to shake it out of you."

Fitzgerald laughed loudly and, pretending to dodge Maggie's menacing hands, swung around and began to sing the second verse,

> "*Then that seahorse,*
> *He did say to me,*
> *Fitzgerald there is a party*
> *On the bottom of the sea.*
> *The King is entertaining,*
> *He'd like it if you'd come*
> *And bring your friend Maggie Muggins,*
> *And anyone else who'd like some fun.*"

Maggie, Petunia, and Grandmother Frog clapped their hands and paws in delight. "We'd all like some fun," said Maggie, "and it will be real fun to go to His Majesty's tea party."

Then Maggie's face fell. "But how do we get there?"

"We ride there, on Gittyep," said Fitzgerald.

"But Gittyep is too small to carry all of us," said Maggie. "He's just one little seahorse, and there's four of us here. Oh dear, oh dear. I wish I'd never heard of the party, because now I want to go, and Gittyep just can't carry us all."

"Oh, don't be such a worry-wart, Maggie Muggins," said the mouse. "It's all arranged. Gittyep is going to bring three other 'Gittyeps' with him. There'll be a seahorse for each of us. So come on!"

They left the house then and hurried down to the seashore. Four little seahorses were waiting in the big breakers that were pounding in over the sands. Maggie was very happy to see her friend Gittyep again.

"It's been such a long time since we've seen each other, Gittyep, and it's so nice of you to think of inviting us to His Majesty's party," said the little girl.

"His Majesty will be very proud to meet you, Maggie Muggins," neighed the little seahorse.

Fitzgerald had something to say about that. "Will he be proud to meet me, too, Gittyep? Because, if he

113

isn't, I'll . . . I'll . . . I'll nibble a hole in his crown."

"You'll do nothing of the sort," said Maggie. And she turned to the little seahorse apologetically. "He doesn't mean it, Gittyep."

The seahorse laughed. "I know he doesn't, because I know Fitzgerald. He likes to hear himself squeak."

Fitzgerald made a funny face, and they all laughed. Then, mounting the seahorses, the four little friends rode away over the waves. The little horses, led by Gittyep, on whom Maggie was seated, headed for the deep sea and out toward the sun. When the shore line was no longer in sight, the horses neighed out a warning that they were going under. Their riders held on tightly, as their seaworthy steeds dived into the green waters of the ocean.

When they reached the sea floor, Maggie cried out in amazement at the beauty around and about. There were sea flowers and sea shells, seaweeds and sea lavender, multicoloured fish and sea urchins on all sides. Suddenly a beautiful pearly castle loomed into sight. Maggie had never seen its like before, and she gasped in admiration. She was about to speak when she heard loud sobbing. It was coming from within the castle. Maggie looked at Gittyep. "It doesn't sound like a very happy tea party," she said to the little seahorse.

Fitzgerald agreed with Maggie, and asked Gittyep who was crying.

"It sounds like His Majesty," said Gittyep. "I wonder what can be the matter?"

"Let's go in, and find out," suggested Maggie.

They went inside and found His Majesty, the King of the Sea, crying his heart out. His head was bare. He was not wearing his crown. When the King saw Gittyep and his guests staring at him in amazement and concern, he pointed toward a big fish who was struggling in the green waters nearby.

The fish was wearing His Majesty's crown, but not on his head. The crown was encircling the body of the fish, like a ring encircles a finger. The crown had pinned down the fins of the fish and he could not swim. It was plain to see that the fish wanted to be free of the crown.

Maggie, bowing in respect before the King, said, "Your Majesty, how did it happen? How did the sea trout get the crown around his body?"

His Majesty, mopping his tears with a filmy handkerchief, said, "I took off my crown to polish it. I was reaching for the polish when the trout came along and swam through the crown and got caught there."

"It was an accident, then?" said Maggie. "He didn't mean to swim through the crown?"

The King shook his head vigorously. "Oh no, he didn't mean to do it. He doesn't want to be inside it. But he can't get out of it. Oh dear, oh dear!"

The King broke into a new flood of tears. Maggie consoled him as best she could, and said that she and her friends would try to help both him and the fish.

"We have hands," she said.

"And paws," added Fitzgerald.

"And paws," smiled Maggie. She took complete charge of the situation then, and told the sea trout to cease his struggling and be still.

"Come, Petunia, Fitzgerald, and Grandmother Frog. We'll all pull on the crown."

They pulled and pulled and pulled. But that crown was wedged on the sea trout so tightly that their efforts were of no avail. The King cried loudly. The fish gasped loudly. Grandmother Frog complained loudly that the salt water was not helping her rheumatism. All in all, it was a very noisy session. Maggie put her hands over her ears so that she might think, and she thought of Mr. McGarrity. She

116

beckoned to Gittyep and told him to carry her back to the shore. She knew that she could get help in the garden. She was gaping like the sea trout when she reached Mr. McGarrity.

He noticed this, and remarked on it. Maggie said in reply to his comments, "No wonder, sir. That's where I've been."

"I don't understand, Maggie," said Mr. McGarrity.

"I've been with a fish. Mr. McGarrity, do you remember the letter that Fitzgerald sent me this morning?"

"I do," said Mr. McGarrity.

"It was an invitation from Gittyep, the seahorse. He asked us to a party at the castle of His Majesty, the King of the Sea. Gittyep and three other sea-horses took us there. Mr. McGarrity, you just should see the bottom of the sea."

"I'm sure it's wonderful," said Mr. McGarrity. "But go on with your story."

"Yes, sir. When we reached the King's pearly castle, he was crying. We went inside to find out what was the matter, and Mr. McGarrity, we found a sea trout wearing His Majesty's crown around his middle."

Mr. McGarrity burst into merry laughter. "Upon my word," he said. "Upon my word. A sea trout with a crown around his middle!"

"Don't laugh, Mr. McGarrity," said the little girl. "It's not funny. The fish's fins are under the crown and he can't swim, and he's not happy. And I pulled and pulled to get him out of the crown, and so did Fitzgerald and Petunia and Grandmother Frog, and then she said her rheumatism was hurting her."

Maggie stopped for breath while Mr. McGarrity bit his lip to keep from further laughter.

"Maggie," he said, "how did it all happen? How did the fish get into the crown?"

Maggie gulped and went on with her story. "His Majesty the King knew that we were coming to visit him, and he wanted his crown to look its very best, so he took it off to polish it, and when he was reaching for the bottle of polish, the sea trout swam by and got caught in the crown."

"It's very sad," said Mr. McGarrity, sympathetically.

"Yes, sir, and please, sir, do you know how to 'un-sad' it?" asked Maggie, looking up hopefully at her faithful friend.

Mr. McGarrity raised his eyebrows. "Maggie Muggins," he said, "you're not asking me how to get the trout out of the crown, are you?"

"Yes, sir, that's what I'm asking," said Maggie. "I can't get the crown off of him. It's on there as tight as a ring, sir."

"A ring, eh?" said Mr. McGarrity. And a smile flashed across his friendly old face. "I have it! Maggie, do you remember the time that your ring was on your finger so tightly that you couldn't get it off?"

"Yes, sir."

"And how did you finally get it off? Do you remember that?" asked the old man.

"Yes, sir," said Maggie. "I soaped it." And a wide smile spread over Maggie's face too.

"Mr. McGarrity," she cried. "You mean that I should soap the fish, don't you, sir?" And Mr. McGarrity nodded.

"Is there any soap in the toolshed, sir?"

They went to the toolshed together and found a large cake of white soap in a box on the windowsill. Maggie thanked her ever-helpful friend, and dashed back to the seashore, mounted the waiting Gittyep, and was at the pearly castle of the King of the Sea in a very few minutes.

119

"I'm back," she cried, as she entered the court room of the still weeping King. "Everything's going to be all right. Mr. McGarrity told me what to do." She turned to the struggling fish. "I'm going to soap you, Mr. Seatrout."

Maggie went to work with vim, and in a few minutes the unhappy trout was covered with a soapy foam.

Fitzgerald laughed. "Look at him bubble . . . look at him bubble! Maggie, the crown's getting loose."

"Yes, it is," cried Maggie excitedly. "It's coming off." The crown was slipping. "It's off!" And the crown was in Maggie's hands.

Gittyep galloped about neighing, "Three cheers for Maggie Muggins!"

"Thank you," said Maggie, modestly. "But the cheers should be for Mr. McGarrity."

The soapy sea trout thanked everyone and went on his way. The King placed his crown on his head and they all had tea.

After the party and, after bidding farewell to her friends in the sea, Maggie went back to the garden and Mr. McGarrity.

He knew at once that all was well again.

"Yes, sir," said Maggie. "All is well." She laughed as she thought about it. "You should have seen the sea trout, Mr. McGarrity. He was very bubbly."

"He looked like a bubble pipe, I suppose?" said the old man.

"Yes," said Maggie. "Just like a bubble pipe. I soaped him, and soaped him, and in a few little minutes the crown slid off the fish into my hands. I gave it to the King, and he put it on his head."

"It's really wonderful what a little soap will do for a person," said Mr. McGarrity.

"Yes, isn't it, sir? What would we do without soap?" asked Maggie.

"I don't know, I just don't know," laughed the old man, and then he said, "All in all, Maggie, I'd say you'd had quite a day."

"Yes," said Maggie Muggins, "because tra la, la la, la la, la lown, the King of the Sea almost lost his crown. I don't know what will happen tomorrow."

THE STONE CAT

Mr. McGarrity smiled to himself as he hoed the third row of carrots with his red-handled hoe. He could hear the dancing feet of Maggie Muggins com-

ing toward him.   He pretended not to hear her as
she rounded the currant bushes, singing,

"Tra la, la la, la la, la luggins,
Here comes Maggie, Maggie Muggins,
And I am coming, tra la, la lo,
Just to say hello, hello,
To Mr. McGarrity, and 'hello', sir."

Mr. McGarrity dropped his hoe then, and pretended to be very much surprised at Maggie's arrival
in the carrot bed.   "Well, upon my word," he said,
"if it isn't Maggie Muggins.   Hello yourself, Miss
Muggins, and how are you today?"

"I'm fine, sir," laughed the little girl.   "And,
do you know something?"

Mr. McGarrity puckered his lips and his brow
and said, "I think it would be safer to say 'no' to that.
No!"

"I'll tell you, then.   I'm looking for something,"
said Maggie Muggins.   "Do you think you can find
it for me, Mr. McGarrity?"

"I might find it if I had a clue as to what you
were looking for," said the old man.   "Is it large?   Is
it tall?   Is it short?   Is it small?   Is it round?   Is it
flat?   Does it mieow like a cat?"

Maggie howled with laughter. Mr. McGarrity was such fun. "It's none of those things," she said. "It's an adventure. I'm looking for an adventure."

"Dear me! Dear me! You're not asking an old gaffer like me to worry my poor old head thinking up an adventure for you, are you?"

"Yes, I am," laughed Maggie, dancing around Mr. McGarrity on one foot. "Yes, I am, sir."

"Well, upon my word," said Mr. McGarrity. "This is a situation, indeed! But I'll do the best I can for you. Just wait until I put my thinking cap on." And Mr. McGarrity made pretend to put on a cap while Maggie still hopped and still laughed.

The old man muttered away to himself, and finally snapped his fingers and said, "I have it! I know the very thing."

Maggie came to a sudden stop in her hops and cried, "What, sir? What is the very thing?"

"Just a minute now, Miss Muggins," said Mr. McGarrity. "I have the very thing in my garden basket." And he began to feel around in the large basket that he always kept nearby. He brought out a large bulb and handed it to Maggie.

She turned it over in her hand and looked at it carefully. But there was disappointment in her

124

freckled face. "It . . . it . . . well, sir, it looks like an onion." And she put it under her freckled nose and sniffed. "But it doesn't smell like an onion."

"Does it smell like an adventure, Maggie Muggins?" asked Mr. McGarrity.

"No, sir, but I guess maybe it is an adventure. Is it, Mr. McGarrity?"

"It is, indeed. You have in your hand, Miss Muggins, a lily bulb. A Chinese lily bulb! And if you say the magic words that I shall give you, after you plant the bulb, that is, it will grow before your very eyes into a beautiful flower. That should be an exciting enough adventure for anyone, including you."

Maggie's head was bobbing up and down in agreement as she took another look at the "adventure" she held in her hand. She wasn't quite clear as to what to do with the magic bulb, and she asked Mr. McGarrity where she should plant it.

"Well now," said the old gardener, "because you're going to share your adventure with Fitzgerald Fieldmouse, Petunia 'possum, and your meadow and woodland friends, I'd suggest that you plant the bulb near the mouse's pink house."

"That's a good idea, sir. That's just what I'll do. And now for the magic word, eh, Mr. McGarrity, eh?"

"Oh yes, yes, the magic words! The bulb is useless unless you have the magic words." Mr. McGarrity scratched his head and looked very thoughtful. "I do hope I can remember the words."

"Oh, Mr. McGarrity," cried Maggie in alarm, "you've got to remember them."

A wide smile crept across Mr. McGarrity's face. Maggie sighed in relief. She knew that her friend had remembered the magic words. She listened carefully to him as he went over the words with her. When she was sure that she knew each and every word, she dashed off towards the meadow and to the home of Fitzgerald Fieldmouse. She ran in to her waiting friends and, without even a "Hello" or "How are you", she told the story of the magic lily bulb.

Fitzgerald cocked his tiny head to one side, looked at her sharply, and said, "I don't believe it."

Maggie gasped at his boldness. "Mr. McGarrity always tells the truth, doesn't he, Petunia?" she said, turning to Mrs. 'possum, who was sitting in the rocking chair.

Petunia nodded her head, but she said, "Lan' sake, Honey Chil', I never done hear tell of he talkin' anythin' but truth, but it sho am hard for me to believe that that there onion you has in your hand is goin' for to grow into pretty Chinese lily."

Maggie then grew very indignant. She pulled herself up to her full height and said haughtily, "It is going to grow into a beautiful Chinese lily, because I know the magic words to make it grow, and if you'll just get your little trowel, Fitzgerald Fieldmouse, and come outdoors with me, I'll prove it to you."

Fitzgerald, armed with the little trowel, followed Maggie and Petunia from the house. They found a soft place in the earth and Fitzgerald began to dig. "I'll make the hole for the bulb," he said, "and you plant it." He then went to work with vigour. Soon he had a nice earthy bed ready for the bulb. Maggie set it in, and Fitzgerald covered it.

Maggie then stood aside and began her magic chanting,

> "*Chinese lily, magic bud,*
> *Grow now from your bed of mud.*
> *Grow now, tall and green and bright,*
> *Wear a lily blossom white.*
> *Make this blossom white as snow*
> *So to China we may go.*
> *Ama lama hing hee hoe*
> *Magic Chinese lily, grow!*"

127

The ground beneath them shuddered, and to their amazement, two small green leaves came out of the ground. They straightened themselves and began to grow. Soon a stem showed itself, and it grew up, and up, carrying a bud as it went. And then, before the eyes of the astonished little three, the bud opened slowly and became a beautiful white flower.

Fitzgerald slipped his tiny paw into Petunia's paw, gulped and squeaked, "It grew! It really did grow!"

"I told you it would," said Maggie smugly.

"Lan' sake," gasped Petunia, "it sho is a pretty flower, and it sho 'nough is big. It is tall as a tree and almost big enough for a little house."

Maggie nodded. "That lily is as big as Fitzgerald's house, isn't it?" She turned to the mouse. "Fitzgerald, I'll lift you up and you climb into the flower. You can tell us what it looks like inside."

"All right," said Fitzgerald, "but hold on to me tightly, Maggie Muggins."

Maggie promised that she would, as she lifted Fitzgerald and set him on the outer edge of the big white lily. He cried out in delight as he began to explore the inner depths of the flower.

"Maggie," he cried, "there seems to be a little

door at the bottom of the flower. Let me go and I'll slip down and see if I can open the door."

Maggie released the mouse and he disappeared into the heart of the flower. The little girl was a bit worried, and called out in warning, "Be careful, Fitzgerald, don't forget that this is a magic flower."

"I won't forget," called the mouse in answer, and then he cried. "It is a door. I'm opening it. I'm . . . Ohhhhhhh," and his voice faded from their hearing.

Maggie looked at Petunia, and Petunia looked at Maggie. Fitzgerald was gone. They called his name over and over, but there was no answer.

"Petunia," said Maggie, "we'll have to find out what happened to him. I'll lift you up so that you can see where he has gone."

Petunia agreed to investigate. Maggie lifted her to the lily blossom. "Lan' sake," she cried excitedly, "there sho 'nough is little door and a little green road down through the stem. I'll go to the doorway and . . . Ohhhhhhh . . ." And Petunia's voice faded.

Petunia had disappeared, too. Maggie called frantically to the 'possum, but Petunia did not answer either. Maggie raced to the back of the mouse's house and dragged the little ladder that hung there to the lily plant. She leaned it against the heavy stem and climbed up into the bud, and straightway slid down through the green stem of the flower. She landed at the waiting Petunia's feet. When Maggie recovered from her quick slide she scrambled to her feet and looked about her. It was a beautiful place. Silver bridges arched themselves over silver streams. Cherry trees in full blossom grew everywhere. And huge flowers guarded the pathways in soldier-like splendour. A giant stone cat, with flashing green jewelled eyes, sat at the end of the bordered roadway. Maggie looked up at the cat in wonder. And then she thought of the mouse. She turned to Petunia and said anxiously, "Where is Fitzgerald?"

"Lan' sake, Honey Chil', I jus' this minute think of that honey mouse. I done slide down here so quick I done got no time for to think of anythin'," said Mrs. 'possum.

"We know he is down here," said Maggie. "Where do you suppose he could have gotten so quickly? I'll call him." And she did. She called and called, but Fitzgerald made no reply. As she turned again to Petunia to discuss the mysterious disappearance of the mouse she found herself looking into the friendly face of a little Chinese boy.

He bowed deeply and said, "If Honourable Maggie-lo-muggaling does search for honourable small mouse-aling, she will find forementioned mouse-aling in bird's nest at far end of garden." The small boy bowed again.

Maggie smiled and thanked the little boy for his help, and then asked, "What is your name, please, and how did Fitzgerald Fieldmouse ever get into a bird's nest?"

"My name," said the boy, "is Mingaling Hingaling, and I see mouse in question leap into honourable bird's nest, in fright."

"In fright?" Maggie gasped. "But why? What frightened him, Mingaling Hingaling?"

The eyes of the little boy twinkled merrily as he smiled and pointed toward the great stone cat with the flashing green jewelled eyes. Maggie shook her head is despair.

"That mouse!" she sighed. "Did you hear what Mingaling Hingaling said, Petunia? Isn't that mouse silly, getting frightened of a stone cat?"

Petunia agreed, but she defended her small friend in the bird's nest. "That sho 'nough is fierce looking cat, Honey Chil'," she said. His eyes am flashin' like green diamonds."

"I know he's a fierce looking cat," said Maggie, "but he's made of stone." And Maggie turned to her new friend, "Mingaling Hingaling, didn't Fitzgerald know that that big cat was made of stone?"

The little boy laughed, "Honourable mouse in question, did not wait to discover that honourable cat was made of stone. Mouse in question leap squealaling into tree-aling."

Maggie sighed again. "Mingaling Hingaling, will you point out the tree in which our silly mouse is hiding?"

The little Chinese boy was happy to do this, and Maggie and Petunia went toward the cherry tree at the far end of the garden. Maggie called out loudly, "Fitzgerald, I know where you are, and I want you to answer me. Get your head out of that nest and listen to me."

Two tiny ears, followed by two beady eyes, showed themselves above the edge of the nest, and a voice followed saying, "I'm listening, but I'm not coming down there."

"Fitzgerald," said Maggie sternly, "you're acting very silly. The very idea of a mouse hiding in a bird's nest!"

"Shame on honey mouse," called Petunia, "running away from cat made of stone!"

Fitzgerald made no reply and Maggie, changing her tone, said softly, "Come on down, Fitzgerald. That big cat is not alive. He's made of stone."

"Like fun he is," answered Fitzgerald. "He growled at me, and he smacked his lips, and he flashed his eyes."

"You're just imagining things, Fitzgerald," said Maggie.

"Oh, so now I'm imagining things," said Fitzgerald indignantly from his bird's nest.

"Yes, you are," said Maggie. "Come right down here, this minute."

But no amount of coaxing would move Fitzgerald Fieldmouse from the safety of the bird's nest, and the stone cat's green eyes kept flashing hungrily in the Chinese sunlight. Maggie knew that it would be of no use to climb the tree to get Fitzgerald. He was too swift for her. He'd leap to another tree when she got near to him. She knew that there was but one thing to do, and that was to seek the advice of Mr. McGarrity. She climbed up the green stem of the lily, leapt to the ground from its flower and went rushing to the garden of her old friend. He looked up from his work when he saw her coming, and said, "Well, upon my word, Maggie Muggins, what is the matter with you? You're falling all over yourself."

"No wonder, sir," said the little girl, "I came back from China, so quickly."

Mr. McGarrity raised his eyebrows, "Oh, you've been to China? I take it the magic lily bulb grew?"

"Yes, sir, and I wish it hadn't," said Maggie Muggins. Mr. McGarrity looked at her in surprise. "I do, sir, honest I do! It would have all been so wonderful if Fitzgerald hadn't gone down first and seen the cat."

"What's this, what's this?" said Mr. McGarrity. "You don't mean to tell me that a Chinese cat has caught Fitzgerald? That is too bad. I'm very sorry! Very sorry, indeed!"

Maggie then explained the situation to Mr. McGarrity, and that gentleman was truly amazed at the story.

"A stone cat!" he gasped. "Well, upon my word."

"And his eyes are green jewels, sir, and they're flashing in the sunlight, and Fitzgerald thinks he's a real cat, and he won't come out of the bird's nest."

Mr. McGarrity roared with laughter at the thought of Fitzgerald in a bird's nest, but realizing that Maggie saw nothing funny in the idea, he said,

134

"Maggie, are you sure that Fitzgerald is in the bird's nest?"

"Yes, sir, I am," said the little girl. "Mingaling Hingaling (he's a nice little Chinese boy that I met) told me so, and besides that, I saw Fitzgerald's ears and eyes sticking out and, besides that, I talked to him. Mr. McGarrity, we all told him that the cat was made of stone but he just wouldn't believe it. He even said the cat growled at him."

Mr McGarrity shook his head. "He's letting his imagination run away with him."

"That's just what I told him, sir, but he didn't believe that either, and how am I going to get him home?"

"Play along with him, Maggie," said the old man promptly. "Yes, that's just what to do! Play along with him. Take a goodly amount of rope from the toolshed. Show it to Fitzgerald. Tell him that you're going to tie up the big cat. When Fitzgerald knows that the cat can't move, he'll run for it."

Maggie's eyes were as wide as saucers as she listened. "But, Mr. McGarrity, it's all so silly. That cat can't touch the mouse."

"I know, I know," said the old man, "but Fitzgerald has his head full of silly fears, and nothing will

135

change his thinking. You do what I say. Mingaling Hingaling will help you to tie up the cat, I'm sure."

Maggie nodded and laughed. "I'll do it, sir," she said, as she raced towards the toolshed for the rope.

The stone cat was still sitting quietly on his pedestal when Maggie arrived back in the magic garden. She told Mingaling Hingaling and Petunia of Mr. McGarrity's plan. They laughed and agreed to help her see it through. Together they bound the cat, paw and foot.

"Run for it, Fitzgerald," cried Maggie, "Run for it."

There was a flash of grey through the garden, and the grey flash was a scampering mouse. Fitzgerald Fieldmouse was in the meadow again in his little pink house.

Maggie Muggins thanked Mingaling Hingaling for his friendly aid, and with Petunia, climbed up the stem again. They went to the mouse's house.

"Fitzgerald Fieldmouse," said Maggie, as she entered the living room, "aren't you ashamed of yourself?"

Fitzgerald roared with mischievous laughter as he said, "Wouldn't you like to know?"

136

Maggie looked at the mouse and was puzzled. Had he been teasing them in the garden? Was he or was he not afraid of the cat?

She was still puzzled when she went back to the garden and Mr. McGarrity.

"Hello, Maggie," said her old friend, "did you get Fitzgerald safely home again?"

"Yes, sir," said the little girl. "And when I asked him if he were not ashamed of himself, he laughed and said 'wouldn't you like to know?' Mr. McGarrity, I don't know what to make of it."

"Then I'd forget it," said Mr. McGarrity. "All in all, Maggie, I'd say you'd had quite a day."

"Yes," said Maggie, "because tra la, la la, la la, la lest, Fitzgerald jumped into a little bird's nest. I don't know what will happen tomorrow."

THE TORN BOOK

Maggie Muggins was laughing as she ran toward the garden and Mr. McGarrity. Her red pigtails were flapping up and down as she ran, and her blue eyes were twinkling merrily as she sang,

138

"Tra la, la la, la la, la lee,
Here comes Maggie Muggins me,
And I am coming, tra la, la lo,
Just to say 'hello, hello' to Mr.
  McGarrity,
And hello, Mr. McGarrity."

Her old friend in the garden smiled as he looked up from his work in the carrot bed. "Hello, yourself, Maggie Muggins," he said, "and how are you today?"

"I'm fine," answered the little girl, "that is, I'm all fine but my head, and it's empty."

Mr. McGarrity laughed as he said, "No!"

"Yes, sir, it's empty," said Maggie Muggins, smiling back at her good friend. "There's not one thing in my head this morning, and what are you going to do about it, Mr. McGarrity?"

"What am I going to do about it?" asked the old gardener in surprise. "You're not asking me that, are you, Maggie?"

"Yes, sir, I am," said Maggie. "I brought my head over here with me so that you could fill it up with things."

Maggie pulled a tender carrot from the dark earth then and, scraping the mud from it with its

139

green fern-like leaves, she began to nibble as she waited for Mr. McGarrity to speak. He stood staring at her. She did bring so many problems to him and today she'd brought an empty head.

He scratched his own head in thought as he muttered, "Dear me, dear me! It is quite a chore you've set for me, Miss Muggins. But I'll see what I can do. What sort of things do you wish me to put in this empty head of yours?"

"Oh, adventures and fun," mumbled Maggie, chewing away happily on her carrot. "It's a nice day, and it does seem a shame to have an empty head on a nice day."

Mr. McGarrity laughed again. He couldn't help it. What a child this was! He agreed with Maggie through his laughter, and asked if she were sure that her red head was completely empty.

"Oh yes, sir. I'm sure. I think a goblin came in the night and gobbled up all my ideas." She pulled another carrot from the ground.

"But perhaps you don't need to worry about the goblin's theft. Perhaps your friend Fitzgerald Fieldmouse will be brimming over with ideas today," said Mr. McGarrity.

Maggie shook her head. "I don't think so, and

do you know the because-why?" Mr. McGarrity didn't know the "because-why". And Maggie went on, "I was talking to him on the telephone before I left the house, and he told me that he was feeling lazy today, and when you're feeling lazy you're not able to think up adventures."

"Very true, and I can understand how he feels, too." And Mr. McGarrity yawned widely. "I'm feeling a bit lazy myself. 'Ho hum.'" He yawned again.

Maggie yawned. "Oh, Mr. McGarrity! Now you've got me yawning, too. Now I feel so lazy that I don't feel like having the adventures that you're going to think up, after you get over being lazy yourself."

Mr. McGarrity yawned again, and snapped his fingers. "I have it, Maggie. I know just what you should do. Have a lazy day."

"All right," said Maggie, "but how do you do it? How do you have a lazy day?"

"You read," said her friend. "Your old 'Mother Goose Book' is in the toolshed, behind the tool chest."

"You mean the one with the big pictures in it?" asked Maggie.

"Yes," said Mr. McGarrity. "I saw it there yesterday. It's quite battered and torn, and when I saw the shape it was in, I couldn't help being a bit dis-

141

appointed in you, Miss Muggins. I thought you were
the kind of little girl who respected books . . . who
looked upon them as good friends."

"And I do, sir. I do. Honest, I do. But don't
you remember how my Mother Goose Book got torn?
A little dog ran off with it one day, and when I caught
him he had chewed the corners off most every page,
and he'd torn some of the pictures, too. Don't you
remember that, Mr. McGarrity?" asked Maggie,
anxiously.

"I do remember," said Mr. McGarrity, "and I
beg your pardon for thinking what I did."

"That's all right, sir," said the little girl. "We
all make mistakes sometimes. And now, if you'll
pardon me, I'll go get the book and go off to the
meadows to have a lazy day." Maggie yawned again,
and so did Mr. McGarrity. And they looked at one
another and laughed.

"Yawns are more catching than measles," the
old man said, as Maggie hopped away.

A few minutes later she was entering the pink
mouse house in the meadow. She found Fitzgerald
on the telephone, telling Big Bite Beaver that he was
going to stay home today, because he felt too lazy
to stir outside his own door.

"I feel the same way," said Maggie to the tiny

fellow, as he put the receiver on the hook. She yawned. Fitzgerald yawned, and Petunia 'possum, who was rocking in the rocking chair, yawned too.

"Lan' sake," said that lady, "Ussen should be 'shamed of ussen. What we goin' for to do? Sit 'round yawning all day long?"

"We're going to sit around," said Maggie, "because we're going to play a 'Mother Goose' game with my Mother Goose Book. I thought of the game when I was coming across the meadow. I'll tell you how it's played."

Maggie explained then that she would read the first line of a rhyme, and one of the others would try to finish it.

Fitzgerald and Petunia thought that the game would be fun, and were eager to begin. Maggie suggested that they take the book out-of-doors. Fitzgerald held up a paw to detain them.

"I'm going to sing a song about it before we go. I'm lazy, but I'm never too lazy to sing," he laughed. And, with a mischievous wink, he went to the tiny piano, and he sang,

> *"Maggie, Maggie, I've been thinking*
> *That it would be lots of fun*
> *To take out your 'Mother Goose Book,*
> *And read stories, in the sun.*

"We shall read about Jack Horner,
We shall read about Boy Blue,
And about the girl named Betty,
Who lost her holiday shoe."

Fitzgerald would have gone on with a third verse, but Maggie ran to his side and, clapping her hand over his mouth, said, "No, no more from you. Let me make up a verse."

Fitzgerald, struggling to free himself, said, "All right, all right, but you needn't smother me to do it. I'll let you sing."

His paws fell on the keys again, and Maggie sang her verse,

"We shall read about Bo-Peep too,
Who lost all her sheep one day.
We shall read about Cock Robin.
We'll have lots of fun today."

Maggie then suggested that Petunia 'possum make up a verse, but Petunia shook her head and said, "If ussen goin' for to have that fun you and honey mouse talk about, let's go have it."

Fitzgerald hopped up and down in glee at the idea and said that he could finish any nursery rhyme that Maggie began.

"I know every one in the book," he squealed. "Try me, just try me. I know all the Mother Goose Children."

"All right," laughed Maggie, hugging the book to her, and going toward the door yard. "I'll try you just as soon as we settle down in the grass."

They settled down in the grass and sunshine, and Maggie opened the tattered book and read, " 'Jack Spratt could eat no fat'."

Before she could go farther, Fitzgerald picked up the rhyme and finished it joyfully, shouting, " 'his wife could eat no lean, and so betwixt them both, they licked the platter clean.' Another one, give me another one."

"It's Petunia's turn," said Maggie, and she turned the page and read, " 'Hark, hark, the dogs do bark'."

"Honey chil', I know she! I know she!" cried Petunia. "I finish it. 'Honey beggars am comin' to town, some them wearing rags, some of them wear ing jags, and some of them honey beggars done wear velvet gowns!' "

Maggie rolled over in the grass, laughing. Petunia looked hurt. "It's right, Petunia, but it's not exactly the way it's written in the book. But you said it the way you say everything, and that makes it right."

Petunia had said the rhyme in her own slow 'possum way. And Maggie had liked it, that's why she had laughed.

Fitzgerald reached for the book. "Let me read the first line of one now, Maggie, eh, please?"

Maggie handed the book over to the eager little mouse, who with pleasurable excitement, quickly turned the pages to read, " 'Little Miss Muffet sat on the . . .' " He stopped. His mouth opened and then shut again. He swallowed hard, and shook his head as if he were not believing what he had seen.

"What is it, Fitzgerald?" asked Maggie. "What's the matter?"

"Miss Muffet isn't on the tuffet," said the little mouse. "She's not there. Look!" He passed the book toward Maggie and Petunia. "The Spider's there, but Miss Muffet is gone. All that is left of Miss Muffet are her shoes and bonnet."

Maggie and Petunia leaned forward. Petunia began to cry. Maggie turned and looked at her.

"Why are you crying, Petunia?" she asked.

"Lan' sake, Honey chil', I is crying 'bout poor little Missy Muffet. That spider sittin' there got big grin on his face. He take Missy Muffet away to his den and roll her all up in his spinnin' silk. That what he done do."

Maggie paled and turned to the spider. She shook an angry finger at the quiet grinning spider and said, "Did you do that, Mr. Spider?"

There was no answer, of course. The spider on the page grinned steadily on, while Fitzgerald added to the mystery of Miss Muffet's disappearance by saying, "I don't think that that spider took Miss Muffet. I think it was his grandmother, or one of his cousins or his aunts, who took her away."

The excited, anxious Maggie now agreed with the mouse, and said that she knew just where Grandmother Spider's den was located. "I saw it this morning when I was coming over here," she said. "But I didn't dream that she had poor little Miss Muffet inside with her."

Fitzgerald pulled himself up to his full height, straightened his green tam o'shanter, snapped his braces, and said, "Let us go and save Miss Muffet from the wicked spider."

"Yes," said Maggie. "We'll do it. Forward march!"

And, like soldiers on parade, they started toward the meadow home of the old spider. They had talked themselves into believing that Grandmother Spider had seized the helpless little paper Miss Muffet. They really believed now that the little lady from the nursery rhyme book was in the clutches of the innocent old spinner of webs.

As they neared the funnel of the grass spider, Maggie put her fingers to her lips. They stood very quietly and listened. They heard the whirring of a tiny spinning wheel coming from the dark depths of the white funnel. Maggie nodded her head knowingly toward her friends.

"Do you hear the spinning wheel? Do you hear it? She's spinning a web now to roll around Little Miss Muffet."

They moved closer and looked into the funnel in the grasses. There was no sign of Miss Muffet, but the spinning wheel whirred on in its merry, steady fashion.

Maggie called out loudly and boldly, "Grandmother Spider, we've come for Little Miss Muffet."

The music of the spinning wheel came to an abrupt ending, and from deep in the grasses came the croaking voice of the old spider. "Did someone call me?" she asked.

"Yes," said Maggie, in answer. "I called you. I'm Maggie Muggins. You know me, Grandmother Spider."

"Of course I know you, Maggie. How are you?" called the spider.

"I'm fine, but Little Miss Muffet isn't. Grandmother Spider, we've come for her. Let her out of your den this very minute."

A grey old face appeared then at the mouth of the funnel. "What are you talking about, Maggie Muggins? I've never heard tell of this Miss Muffet of whom you speak."

"Oh, Grandmother Spider, shame on you," said Fitzgerald Fieldmouse. "You have Little Miss Muffet down there in your funnel, and you're spinning a web to roll around her. We heard your spinning wheel."

"Certainly you heard my spinning wheel," said the old lady, now growing angry. "Why shouldn't you hear my spinning wheel. I'm making a little gossamer gown for the Lady Bug. She's going to dance at the Bug Ballet."

Maggie tried to keep calm, but she was clenching her fists in her efforts to do so. "Grandmother Spider," she said, with what seemed great patience, "I'm sorry that I do not believe you. We know that you have Little Miss Muffet in your funnel."

Mrs. Spider shook two of her eight legs at

Maggie. "Don't be ridiculous, Maggie Muggins," she said. "I've always heard that you were fair and kind. But I'm beginning to change my mind. You're downright stupid and unkind to accuse me of something I haven't done. I told you that I had never heard tell of Miss Muffet until you mentioned her name. Now, I'll thank you to go about your business and let me go about mine." And, with that, the irate old spider disappeared again. In another minute the three little friends heard the whirring of the spinning wheel once more.

Maggie looked at the others and sighed. Then she said, "You go home, Fitzgerald and Petunia. I'm going to Mr. McGarrity. He'll know how to save Little Miss Muffet from the spider's den."

And away she ran, leaving her two friends behind her. As she ran towards the old gardener, who was working in the carrot bed, she called, "Mr. McGarrity, please tell me how to get her away from her."

Mr. McGarrity leaned on his red-handled hoe and looked at his little red-headed friend in amazement. When she reached his side he said, "Well, upon my word, this doesn't look like the lazy child who left me a little while ago. What's wrong, Maggie?"

"Everything, sir," puffed Maggie. "Well, that

is, one thing is wrong. Don't you think it's wrong for a spider to take a little girl, all but her shoes and bonnet, and drag her into a spider's den and roll her up in spider silk?"

Maggie looked at Mr. McGarrity expectantly, thinking to find him greatly shocked at the idea. But instead of expressing alarm, he laughed. "It does sound like a dreadful experience," he said. "Who was the little girl? Not Maggie Muggins, I hope."

"No, sir. Not Maggie Muggins! I'm here with you. It's Little Miss Muffet, sir. She's in the spider's den and the spinning wheel is going 'whirr whirr whirr'."

"No," said Mr. McGarrity.

"Yes, sir, Miss Muffet! All that is left of the poor little thing are her shoes and bonnet and, Mr. McGarrity, we went to Grandmother Spider's funnel in the grasses, and she told me to go about my business and she'd go about hers."

"I can't say that I blame her," said Mr. McGarrity.

Maggie gasped. Mr. McGarrity smiled, patted Maggie on the head, and said, "Now, Miss Muggins, don't look so unhappy. Do you know what you've done?"

"No, sir," said Maggie.

151

"You've let your imagination run away with you," said the old man.

"Have I?" said Maggie, puzzled.

"You have, indeed," said Mr. McGarrity. "Maggie, where did you find Little Miss Muffet's bonnet and shoes?"

"In the meadow," said Maggie, "right in front of Fitzgerald's house."

"Maggie, I'm going to ask that question again. Where exactly did you find Miss Muffet's shoes and bonnet? Think now before you answer."

"In the meadow, in the book," said the little girl, and her face turned a bright red. "I found them in the old book. Oh, Mr. McGarrity, I found them on the torn page of the old book."

"Yes. The dog chewed a paper Miss Muffet and left her paper shoes and paper bonnet," said Mr. McGarrity to Maggie Muggins. "Who started all this excitement about the spider's taking Miss Muffet away?"

"Petunia," said Maggie. "She began to cry about poor Little Miss Muffet." Maggie tried to defend herself then, and said, "But Mr. McGarrity, we did hear Grandmother Spider spinning silk."

Mr. McGarrity shook his head. "She may have

been spinning, but she was not making a web in which to roll Miss Muffet. Spider's silk comes from two or three little spinerets inside of their bodies. The spinerets are the shape of tiny fingers. The silk is a liquid, like water. When they want to make a web they send this liquid out of their bodies, and when it comes into the air it hardens and becomes a thread."

Maggie nodded that she understood, and then she told Mr. McGarrity that Grandmother Spider had told them that she was making a gossamer gown for a lady bug.

"And you didn't believe her, Maggie?" asked Mr. McGarrity.

"No, sir, I didn't. I'd let my imagination run away with me so far that I didn't believe. Mr. McGarrity, I'll have to go over there and ask Grandmother Spider to forgive me, won't I?"

"Yes, Maggie, you'll have to do that right away," said Mr. McGarrity.

Maggie left the garden and went straight away to the spider's funnel. She called softly this time, "Grandmother Spider, it's Maggie Muggins again. I've come to tell you that I am sorry for being so rude to you. I truly am, and I hope you'll forgive me."

Grandmother Spider, understanding that children sometimes did let their imaginations run away with them, forgave her readily. Feeling much happier, Maggie went back to the pink mouse house in the meadow to explain all that had happened to her friends.

"It was a paper Miss Muffet that we got all excited about," she said. "And when Petunia cried about the paper Miss Muffet . . ."

"We let our imaginations run away with us," said Fitzgerald Fieldmouse.

"Yes," said Maggie. "How did you know?"

Later, when Maggie was gack in the garden with her old friend, she said, "Grandmother Spider forgave me, and Petunia and Fitzgerald felt just as sad as I did about letting our imaginations run away with us. They went to ask Grandmother Spider's pardon, too. I think she'll forgive them like she forgave me, don't you, Mr. McGarrity."

"I think so, Maggie," said Mr. McGarrity laughingly. "All in all, Maggie," he went on, "you've had quite a day."

"Yes, sir," laughed Maggie Muggins, "because, tra la, la la, la la, la luffet, we thought a spider took Little Miss Muffet. I don't know what will happen tomorrow.